Encounters with Lise
and Other Stories

》》》》》》》》》》   《《《《《《《《《《

Leonid Dobychin

Encounters
with Lise and
Other Stories

EDITED AND WITH AN INTRODUCTION
BY RICHARD C. BORDEN

TRANSLATED FROM THE RUSSIAN
BY RICHARD C. BORDEN
WITH NATALIA BELOVA

NORTHWESTERN UNIVERSITY PRESS
EVANSTON, ILLINOIS

》》》》》》》》》》   《《《《《《《《《《

Northwestern University Press
Evanston, Illinois 60208–4170

Printed in the United States of America

10 9 8 7 6 5 4 3 2 1

ISBN 0–8101-1972–2

Library of Congress Cataloging-in-Publication Data

Dobychin, Leonid.
    [Short stories. English. Selections]
    Encounters with Lise / L. Dobychin ; edited and with an introduction by
Richard C. Borden ; translated from the Russian by Richard C. Borden with
Natalia Belova.
       p. cm. — (European classics)
    Includes bibliographical references.
    ISBN 0-8101-1972-2 (pbk. : alk. paper)
    1. Dobychin, Leonid—Translations into English. I. Borden, Richard C.
(Richard Chandler) II. Belova, Natalia. III. Title. IV. European classics
(Evanston, Ill.)
PG3476.D573A22 2005
891.73'42—dc22

                                        2005001544

»»» CONTENTS «««

Until the 1990s, L. Dobychin was almost entirely unknown out-side the circle of Leningraders who for half a century had pre-served the writer's manuscripts and kept his memory alive. Today, his recognition as a unique and important talent, one of the last and brightest blooms of Russian literary modernism, is secure.[1]

After witnessing the advent of Gorbachev's glasnost and the subsequent fall of the Soviet state, students of Russian culture believed that a parade of unknown manuscripts would emerge, like long-confined gulag prisoners, from the secret drawers to which nonconformist Soviet writers had consigned them for decades. But this anticipation was largely frustrated. This was especially so for readers in the West and among the Russian elites who had long been familiar with the works of writers such as Vladimir Nabokov, Alexander Solzhenitsyn, Mikhail Bulgakov, and Sergei Platonov, all of whom had been exiled, incarcerated, or had their works banned or butchered by the censor. For such readers, there were few surprises. One delightful revelation, however, came with the rediscovery of "L. Dobychin."[2]

Dobychin's idiosyncratic writing, while never broadly known, was highly regarded by such contemporaries as Kornei Chukovsky, Yury Tynyanov, Veniamin Kaverin, and Evgeny Shvarts. Often com-pared with eccentric prodigies such as Bruno Schulz, Paul Gauguin, and Velimir Khlebnikov, Dobychin was an exacting miniaturist. Like Nabokov and Anton Chekhov, he was an artist in the "lesser"

Russian tradition, whose delicately contrived narratives challenge readers to return again and again to wrestle with their subtleties.[3]

Leonid Ivanovich Dobychin was a tragic figure. An awkward and lonely man who died a probable suicide, Dobychin was born in the Latvian city of Dvinsk, today's Daugavpils, in 1894, the son of a doctor who died when the writer was still a boy and a mother who worked as a midwife. Nothing is known of Dobychin's childhood except, perhaps, for what one may extrapolate from his fictional portrayal in *The Town of N* (*Gorod En,* 1935) of a childhood set in a time and place similar to his own. Nor, for that matter, is much known of Dobychin's adult life, other than the brief reminiscences left by Kaverin and Marina Chukovskaia and the glimpses of his life as a writer and social observer that are afforded by the letters he addressed to literary acquaintances.[4]

Like his character Kunst in the story "Farewell," Dobychin was studying at the Polytechnic Institute in St. Petersburg when revolution upended Russian society in 1917. He subsequently worked for most of his life as a poorly paid statistician, living in provincial towns in northern Russia and Latvia and sharing single rooms with his mother, brother, and two sisters. He claimed that, because of his perennial lack of money and a private workspace, he wrote only in summer, out-of-doors, or when he was absent from work due to illness. He did not even have his own writing table until he was forty years old and received a room in a Leningrad communal apartment from the Writers' Union. The conditions under which he created could hardly have been worse. Glimpses may be gleaned from remarks in his correspondence. On December 3, 1924, for example—when Dobychin was just beginning to publish the occasional story in the Soviet press—he wrote to Chukovsky to thank him for a letter and requested that he write again, since the letter had allowed him to feel less like an "office rat." In a letter to his editor, M. L. Slonimsky, on March 15, 1933, he writes:

Nine chapters of my novel [*The Town of N*] have been written, and
when there are ten I'll send them to You. The chapters' composi-
tion is delayed by the absence

a) during the entire winter of electricity,
b) for more than a month of kerosene, as a result of which a short-
age of lighting is experienced, and days off from work are
devoted to standing in lines.

With no literary ties outside the Leningrad publishing world, itself
distant, Dobychin's isolation was acute. When, in a letter of January 17, 1925, Dobychin asks Chukovsky not to get angry because
he pesters him with so many requests to read stories, he explains:
"After all, You are my only reader." On the other hand, Dobychin
disputed any suggestions of literary influence and asserted that he
was impervious to criticism, since he wrote the only way he knew
how and had no intention of writing otherwise. He dismissed all
comparisons made between his writing and that of others, especially obvious candidates such as Tynyanov, Mikhail Zoshchenko,
and the Oberiu absurdist Daniil Kharms.[5] While he did single out
the work of several contemporaries—Isaac Babel, Tynyanov,
Yevgeny Zamyatin, Zoshchenko—for measured praise, he had a
reputation as a caustic critic. And while he regarded himself as
fully independent, he was to have been included in an anthology of
Oberiu-related writing that never appeared, together with the likes
of Kaverin, Tynyanov, Yury Olesha, and Victor Shklovsky, who,
while not part of the Oberiu circle, were deemed to be aesthetically
and spiritually akin.[6]

Despite Dobychin's undeniable originality, some of the defining
traits of his art may be less sui generis than idiosyncratic variations
of practices shared by contemporaries. Zoshchenko's radical con-
cision; Zoshchenko's and Platonov's attempts to capture the
grotesque nuances of speech and thought that were developing

among the newly literate and politically conscious Soviet masses; the dark humor of Zoshchenko, Tynyanov, and Platonov; and Kharms's syntax of the absurd all come to mind.[7]

A more compelling case for comparison, however, may be to non-Russian modernists such as James Joyce, especially his *Dubliners* (1914) stories, and Virginia Woolf. Some of Dobychin's harshest critics, in fact, adduced the affinity with Joyce as opprobrium. In recent years, the comparison has been touted by Dobychin's admirers, such as writers Andrei Bitov and Victor Erofeyev, as a token of praise.[8]

In what he called his "second career"—writing—Dobychin managed to publish two slight volumes of laconic stories and one novel. The story collections, *Encounters with Lise* (*Vstrechi s Liz*) and *The Portrait* (*Portret*), published in small editions in 1927 and 1931, respectively, were met with official silence, except for a pair of reviews, one harsh, the other a mix of muted praise and reproval.[9] In any event, the stories' complexity and their comic portrayal of post-Revolutionary Russia guaranteed their obscurity among Soviet readers at large. Before *The Town of N* could find its readership, both the book and its author had vanished.[10]

When Dobychin received his room in Leningrad, he was free at last to pursue writing full time. It appears that he was also directing his art along a new path at that juncture, moving away from the miniature and the modernistic to a more expansive and dark social realism. This shift apparently arose under the influence of his new neighbor, a peasant who regaled the writer with tales of life as a *bezprizornik*, one of the millions of homeless orphans who had roamed the Russian countryside in the first years after the Revolution. The fruits of this new subject and stylistic orientation—the grimly comical "Savages" (*Dikie*, 1934–36?; first published in 1989) and the shocking *Shurka's Kin* (*Shurkina rodnia*, 1936?; first published in 1993), which Erofeyev selected as his "International

Book of the Year" in 1994—suggest that Dobychin was just beginning to explore the spectrum of his gifts when the publication of *The Town of N* in 1935 triggered his demise.[11]

The Town of N is both a lyrical exploration of childhood myth-making, set in the Russian provinces at the turn of the century, and a satirical indictment of society at that time. Like the original "N"—the setting of Nikolai Gogol's *Dead Souls* (1842), from which Dobychin takes his title—Dobychin's town is something of a spiritual wasteland, populated by citizens who are bigoted, smug, and mean. Through his title, Dobychin suggests that his characters are latter-day counterparts to Gogol's cast of rogues and buffoons.

Soviet critics attacked Dobychin's novel for its "formalist" style at a time when formalism was, in the eyes of the state, anathema. Critics also observed that this ostensible formalism was grafted onto a "decadent" view of humanity. By linking Gogol's provincial Russia at the beginning of the nineteenth century with the Russia portrayed in *The Town of N* a century later, and by implying that little had changed in social and human nature, Dobychin, it was suggested, demonstrated skepticism about the Marxist understanding of society's inescapable advance through historical processes. This contention was supported by the fact that Dobychin's stories, published earlier, had portrayed a place similar to "N" that was explicitly Soviet, wherein the new system and ideology had created nothing but a peculiar new coloring for the same essential bleakness.

On January 28, 1936, a few months after *The Town of N*'s appearance, Stalin's infamous attack on Dmitry Shostakovich's modernistic music initiated a campaign against "formalism" in all the arts. At a meeting of the Leningrad Writers' Union shortly thereafter, Dobychin, perhaps because of his obscurity and lack of patronage, perhaps due to his presumed homosexuality, was singled out as the first "whipping boy"—the chief "formalist"—

among Leningrad writers. Dobychin's assailants accused him, absurdly, of sharing his fictional characters' views, notably those of his child protagonist in *The Town of N*, whose (literally) nearsighted vision of society was cast as a reflection of Dobychin's political nearsightedness. Dobychin was appalled by this willful misreading of his book and by unsubtle hints that he was a class enemy. He responded only by stating that he could not agree with what had been said; he then departed. He disappeared the next day, after confiding plans to kill himself to an acquaintance—who later proved to have been a police spy. Dobychin was never seen again.

Dobychin's stories began finding their way back into print in the late 1980s. After a decade of republications and the debuts of previously unpublished work, Dobychin has achieved a stature such that Erofeyev could write, as early as 1994: "Ten years ago, no one knew [him]. Now he is one of the main heroes of twentieth-century Russian literature. His name—Leonid Dobychin. Not even the author of *The Master and Margarita*, Mikhail Bulgakov, enjoyed such a rapid posthumous ascent of the literary Olympus."[12] Elsewhere, Erofeyev has testified to Dobychin's influence, along with other "previously unknown" writers such as Nabokov, Jorge Borges, and Ezra Pound, on the "alternative" stream in Russian fiction today.[13] Five volumes of criticism devoted to Dobychin's writing have appeared, and his fiction has been translated widely.[14]

Not unlike Dobychin's first critics, readers at first may find that nothing much happens in these stories: they are very laconic, seemingly plotless, and sometimes read like a string of loosely linked telegrams. Closer study, however, reveals them to be incisive, ironical snapshots of human foibles and social farce, concise explorations of romantic misadventure and illusion, political and religious inanity, hypocrisy and delusion. Sense is almost never rendered explicitly in Dobychin's stories, and "meaning" is never explained nor express judgment passed. Rather, what actually transpires and what is significant behind the poker face of Dobychin's narrative is revealed by ironical juxtaposition, context, allusion, structure, and style alone. Again, in all this, Dobychin's stories recall none so much as Joyce's *Dubliners*.[15]

As noted, Joyce's is the name most frequently associated with Dobychin. While Dobychin's stories do resemble Joyce's in a number of important ways, no broad comparison to any writer would speak adequately to either artist's unique creation. Nevertheless, selective comparison to Joyce—one of the most scrutinized of writers—offers perspective.

Joyce's *Dubliners* and Dobychin's *Encounters with Lise* and *The Portrait* were all at first widely misread. They were regarded as sketches, naturalistic slices of life—not complex, meticulously crafted tales in which each detail proves indispensable to the whole. The integrity of both authors' stories, due to their originality, required protection from uncomprehending editors and printers.

Joyce and Dobychin both inscribe within their fictions "a chapter of the moral history" of their respective nations.[16] Many of Joyce's Dubliners and Dobychin's neophyte Soviets are creatures who yearn to escape the banality of their lives, but remain ineluctably confined. Both writers define their nations—Joyce explicitly, Dobychin implicitly—as wallowing in states of spiritual and social paralysis. Dobychin's vision of Soviet social paralysis, however, is highly ironical, for that paralysis exists within a context of revolution, wherein all the rhetoric and ritual and all the fundamental social and philosophical assumptions may be brand new and radically different from the old, yet nonetheless prove in their consequence to be no more than a meretricious guise for the same tired story.

Each author writes "in a style of scrupulous meanness and with the conviction that he is a very bold man who dares to alter in the presentment, still more to deform, whatever he has seen and heard." For both, such "scrupulous meanness" defines not only the unsentimental, unsparing spirit in which they examine their respective societies, but also their stylistic economy and their investment of an electrical charge in the smallest details—a charge that may illuminate the whole.[17]

Like Joyce's *Dubliners,* Dobychin's stories are linked by recurring themes and motifs. In Dobychin's case, these include the world of the "cinematograph"—the movies of Mary Pickford and other stars of the silver screen that provide Dobychin's provincials with their sense of the romantic, the poetical, and the exotic, glimpses of which make them "long for the extraordinary, to go away somewhere, be a cinema actor or a pilot." This longing itself becomes an important motif. Dobychin's characters thirst for "evenings full of poetry," "a beautiful garden," "Venezia e Napoli." Not only are faraway places such as America and the Transvaal invoked as symbols of the mysterious and the unobtainable, but so are such nearby loci as Leningrad, with its Admiralty and Winter Palace, and even neighboring Courland Province. Far from attaining such romance, however, Dobychin's Soviets find themselves bound to a world of barracks and purges, culture palaces and rapprochements, trade union congresses and antireligion campaigns, politically correct magic tricks and propagandistic horticulture.

Dobychin's Soviet landscape is also defined by a cornucopia of corpses, funerals, and cemeteries. This intrusion of old-fashioned mortality onto the political scene causes, as it were, an ironical metaphysical rain to fall on the Soviet parade.[18] In fact, between all the funeral processions that wend their way through Dobychin's tales and the endless state-sponsored rallies and manifestations,

Dobychin's Soviets spend an inordinate amount of time marching. It is at the intersection of these two very different types of "parade"—the political and the spiritual—that Dobychin's ironical parade crosses readers' paths.[19]

Like Joyce, Dobychin organizes his stories around a sort of secular "epiphany," Joyce's term for a moment "of expression that, perfect in its wholeness and harmony, will show forth in an instant of illumination a meaning and significance greater than the words in another combination would carry."[20] Dobychin, like Joyce, builds his narratives around "an apparently trivial incident, action, or single detail which differs from the others making up the story only in that it illuminates them, integrates them, and gives them meaning."[21] Dobychin's "Yerygin," for example, concludes with back-to-back epiphanies. One epiphany illuminates the character and one the reader, and the two combined create an ironical banner for Dobychin's parade. The epiphany for the eponymous character, who for months has sought a felicitous theme for the Soviet fiction he aspires to write, arrives first. Yerygin's "epiphany" is sparked by the sight of stalks of hay trailing from a cart and tracing a pattern in the snow, which reminds him of how the hairs on his leg had traced lines in the sand the previous summer. Somehow this accidental symmetry propels Yerygin's random experiences, fantasies, and observations of the previous months into alignment, transfigured into potential narrative fiction. Now Yerygin is inspired to create. The reader's epiphany ensues when Yerygin's prospective chef d'oeuvre proves to be a ridiculous paradigm of the Soviet revolutionary potboiler. The delicate structure of Dobychin's story only satirizes his character's crude contrivance all the more.

In "The Nurse," readers confront another "epiphany" after following the central character, Mukhin, through a typical day in the new Soviet life. After playing soccer, Mukhin watches a parade, attends the unveiling of a monument to a fallen Communist (during which he spots the attractive nurse), witnesses the funeral procession of a young woman who has committed suicide after expulsion from the Communist Party Youth League, and overhears praise of the suicide's friend, who, while howling with grief, displays Communist discipline by not joining the religious procession. Later, Mukhin reads about the memorial unveiling in the newspaper while sitting beneath a schedule for political education. He overhears people sing a jingle from a social cleanliness campaign and joins acquaintances for a beer at the Mosselprom cafeteria. There the story ends, with Mukhin announcing, in words that seem perfectly banal, yet which illuminate all that has preceded them: "I almost got to meet the nurse." This fact constitutes the high point and final significance of Mukhin's day, and in these simple words the notion that revolution has fundamentally reconfigured the world, radically transforming both Russian society and the new Soviet individual, is exposed as fatuous. All the Soviet pomp and circumstance that ostensibly structured Mukhin's day is unveiled as so much twaddle. For, when the day is done, the fact that a man almost met a woman triumphantly obscures the state's designs on that man's soul. It is in part because they structure their narratives around such compact "epiphanies" that Dobychin and Joyce raised narrative economy to such heights.[22]

Dobychin unmasks early Soviet society as an absurdist wonderland. He delineates a world of aspiring poets from the ranks of the barely literate, of naive political enthusiasm standing shoulder to shoulder with cynical timeserving, political denunciation, and sumptuous vulgarity. He discloses a land where ubiquitous acronyms and journalistic cliché disfigure the mother tongue, a world of half-digested rhetoric from newly minted ideologues. This brave new world is a locus of misguided platitudes, monstrous neologisms, and general confusion. Dobychin's is a land of flowerbeds honoring "the leaders," of penal battalions spelling out "Proletariat of all nations, unite!" with bricks on a bed of sand. It is a world in which "cavaliers" dance with "cavaliers" while the women stand by, frustrated. It is a charming, often comical parade of human folly.

Dobychin, like Joyce, focused his social vision on the yawning gap between pretense, discourse, and reality. In Dobychin's case, ironical "parades" arise from the juxtaposition of the new Soviet reality with eternal verities. The contrapuntal dance between these disparate worlds reveals a complete miscarriage in the mutual assimilation of vision and value. In his *Dubliners*, Joyce held a mirror up to Irish society to disclose life as it truly was behind the false communion dispensed by church and state. Dobychin held a mirror up to Soviet culture to expose the human truths behind the surface of revolutionary rhetoric and ritual. Both authors, in a sense, realized these thematics by means of narrative form. It might, indeed, be argued that it was this shared social vision that engendered their similar narrative strategies. Just as their stories explore the discrepancy between appearances, discourse, and reality, so are they constructed to appear on the surface to be transparent sketches, and yet they reveal hidden complexity, integrity, and significance when dissected for subtext and irony.

This juxtaposition of Soviet pomp with eternal verities also generates much of Dobychin's subversive humor. In the story "Encounters with Lise," for example, an involuntary reflex by one character juxtaposes a decadent novel by Octave Mirbeau entitled *Torture Garden* (1899) with the local Soviet pleasure garden named for Karl Marx and Friedrich Engels, ironically implying some commonality between the two. In the same story, readers find the bourgeois protagonist, who is cultivating sympathy for the revolution as a means of ingratiating himself with his Communist boss, sunning himself at the shore with a friend. This friend's free association bonds together two highly incongruous components, relegating them to the same level of importance: "Working people of all nations . . . await their emancipation. Take a look, please, has it gotten red enough yet between my shoulder blades?" This is just one of many instances in which a morsel of official cant finds itself isolated within an everyday context, engulfed by everyday speech and concern and thereby rendered absurd.

A related mode of irony arises in "Kozlova," in which Dobychin portrays three office workers:

> They were sitting doing overtime. Flies were biting. A big bell droned, and, tinkling, the windowpanes joined it.
>
> Demeshchenko had bent over the table and was scratching out "Comrade Lenin."
>
> Garashchenko and Kalegaeva, lounging on chairs, were gnawing sunflower seeds and gawking at the new [coworker].

By bracketing these two forms of "overtime," the narrative inadvertently, as it were, equates the perpetuation of Comrade Lenin's cause with gawking and the gnawing of seeds.

Dobychin's characters prove adept at raining ironical diminution upon their own heads as well. Our sympathies for Sorokina and her fantasies about some "Vanya" in the story "Dorian Gray," for example, are dampened by her failure to extend her imagination beyond the nomenclatural confines of state propaganda:

> She'd take him by the hand, and he'd lead her away.
>
> "We'll go for a boat ride. I have a boat, the *Sun-Yat-sen*."

Dobychin's comedic inspiration likewise is not entirely dependent on Soviet hypocrisies and absurdities. Human nature alone provides plenty of material for satire. In "Kozlova," for example, the new "girl" in the office advises her coworkers that if they should ever quarrel with someone, they should "pray to John the Warrior.

I always do, and you know, she was taken away and sentenced to three years." The episode's "epiphany" arrives with Kozlova's response to this noisome counsel: "A good woman," thought Kozlova, "religious . . . ."

Dobychin charges readers with the responsibility of descrying his ironical parades themselves. He entrusts readers to discover those epiphanies in which he, as it were, winks at them from over his characters' shoulders. He invites readers to become fellow marchers in his ironical parade and plumb comic mysteries such as the state's campaign to swaddle its citizens, accustomed to bathing in the buff, in short pants before they dip into the waters of life. He bids readers to explore the societal faults along which the state's temporal parades intersect the timeless parades of love and death.[23]

Much has been made of Dobychin's stylistic "neutrality" and "simplicity." Dobychin's narratives may, indeed, be brief and sparse, but his sentence and paragraph structures contain myriad subtleties, not all of which are fully transferable into English.[24] Characteristic features include sentences that are either short and staccato or long and jolting. The former include sentences such as these from "Yerygin":

> The bazaar was big. A stench hung in the air. Chinese were doing conjuring tricks. Metric tables were suspended on stalls.

The Russian renders this staccato even more effectively, since its sentences comprise fewer words. Such writing in part reflects the principles of expressive and constructive editing that were then developing in cinematic montage. Cinema stood at the avant-garde of early Soviet culture, and the theories and practices of Sergei Eisenstein, Vsevolod Pudovkin, Lev Kuleshov, and Dziga Vertov influenced other art forms. The self-contained, separate pictures

Dobychin produces in each short sentence create an effect similar to narrative montage—a series of spliced-together frames that represent a multidimensional environment from a multiplicity of perspectives. One such "montage" is this passage from "Savkina":

> The sun warmed the back of one's head. Wagons rattled. Conceited rich dames Frumkina and Fradkina strolled. Morkovnikova, shaded by bottles, watched from her kiosk. Trumpets sparkling, a funeral march played. Wreaths of pine branches and black flags were being carried. In a red coffin carted upon a curtained hearse was Olympia Kukel.

Again, the Russian, with its superior economy, creates this effect more dramatically.

Representing Dobychin's second sentence type, in which the reader reaches a subject and predicate only after a long windup of qualification, is this introduction to the title character of "Encounters with Lise":

> Wriggling her shoulders as she went, head lifted high, with a triumphant smile on her face, violet with powder, Lise Kuritsyna turned off German Revolution Street onto Third International Street.

Sometimes Dobychin places a broad expanse of qualification between a subject and its predicate or a verb and its object, such as in this sentence from the same story:

> The penals, creeping in a squatting position, painstakingly wrote out with little bricks on a strip alongside the battalion, spread with sand, "Proletariat of all nations, unite!"

A rendering such as this may recreate Dobychin's syntactical tightrope-walking rather closely, but it does not make for graceful style. The present translation, however, imitates the original as closely as possible whenever the resulting English is not too unreasonable. Thus, this sentence from "Lidiya" retains its original peculiarity:

> The Youth Leader, thickset, without any belt, barefoot, brandishing a switch, was dispatching a billy goat out onto the street.

Dobychin also sometimes sets a series of staccato phrases between two verbs joined by "and":

> Seleznyova locked the gate and, wearing a kerchief, tucking her hands into her cuffs, stooped over, squat, in a long skirt and felt boots, set out. ("As You Wish")

On other occasions, Dobychin stands a predicate adjective far from its subject:

> Guests knocked and, unfastening the muskrat around their necks, squat, joyously looked up at us from down below. ("The Portrait")

Such stylistics constitute a strategy by which the writer, to use Shklovsky's formalist concept, "retards" the reading process and keeps his reader off-kilter, forced to notice each detail.

Dobychin's proclivity for dropping sentences' subject pronouns, such that verbs stand alone, is another important idiosyncrasy. In part because a Russian verb has number and gender markers, a subject pronoun need not always front the predicate of a Russian sentence. English's dearth of number markers for verbs, and of gender markers for nouns, adjectives, and verbs, means that to translate this particular signature of Dobychin's style is not always possible. In "The Nurse," for example, Dobychin presents a narrative in which the subject is often only implied. Again and again the reader encounters sentences such as "Finally set forth," and "Forming up on Victims' Square." Cumulatively, this lack of explicit subjects suggests an absence of real people, or an anonymous mass moving about mechanically, a troupe of puppets rehearsing empty gestures. It is not always possible to reproduce this effect in translation without obscuring narrative sense.

The Russian language possesses a far greater capacity for forming diminutives than does English, and the employment of diminutives, especially in colloquial speech, can be incomparably greater. Diminutives in Russian are formed most frequently by adding a suffix to a word or name. They may express not only actual smallness in size, but also an imputed smallness in token of affection, disparagement, scorn, or condescension. Dobychin employs diminutives copiously, often ironically, for comic effect. This stylistic feature too is not always transferable to English without an unbecoming glut of modifiers such as "little," "small," and "dear."

Another stylistic idiosyncrasy is Dobychin's frequent reversal of conventional sentence structure. Rather than a commonplace construction such as, "A wet wind flew through the open windows," Dobychin often has it, "Through the open windows blew a wet wind." This reversal of the subject-predicate structure is more common in Russian than in English, but Dobychin's "abuse" of it causes many sentences to stand apart, awkwardly, as distinct pictures, and forces the reader off balance, unable to assimilate narrative flow automatically. Dobychin compels readers to attend each word by, so to speak, crisscrossing his narrative paths with syntactical speed bumps. Again, the translation retains this feature frequently, but not always, due to its more limited viability in English stylistics.

Other peculiarities include Dobychin's deflation of conclusions to his sentences, leaving verbs that normally require qualification standing naked. In "Konopatchikova," for example, we find: "Polushalchikova came from the kitchen and, taking pride, stood." Stood how? Stood where? Stood why? There is something both comical and disturbing in this narrative flatness, this faux-naïveté, as though it reflects the vacuity and limited horizons of Dobychin's provincials. In a related vein, Dobychin, following Gogol, compiles lists of incompatibles or creates unexpected, absurd combinations, such as this from "Konopatchikova":

> They conversed in a low voice and smiled sadly: Konopatchikova, wearing a woolen beret with a little tassel; Vdovkin, broad-shoul-dered and nose-blowing; and Beryozynkina, meek, with a small head.

The translation endeavors to preserve as much of this stylistic originality as possible.

Notes

This volume contains all of the stories that were published in Dobychin's lifetime, in the collections *Encounters with Lise* (1927) and *The Portrait* (1931). It also includes two stories, "Old Ladies in a Small Town" and "Ninon," that were not published until 1988 and 1989, respectively. Though they are not in any sense defined by a Soviet zeitgeist—"Old Ladies in a Small Town" is set on the eve of World War I and "Ninon" at an indeterminable time—these stories are much akin to the others included here in style, narrative strategy, and theme.

1. "L. Dobychin" was how Leonid Ivanovich Dobychin (1894–1936?) requested that his publications be attributed. See V. S. Bakhtin, "Pod igom dobrykh nachal'nikov: Sud'ba i knigi pisatelia L. Dobychina," in *L. Dobychin: Polnoe sobranie sochinenii i pisem*, ed. V. S. Bakhtin, A. F. Belousov, and A. K. Slavinskaia (St. Petersburg: AOZT "Zhurnal 'Zvezda,'" 1999), 19 (hereafter cited as *Dobychin-99*).

2. Information about Dobychin's life and works may be found in Bakhtin, "Pod igom dobrykh nachal'nikov," in *Dobychin-99*, 7–44, and "Dobychin: Shtrikhi zhizni i tvorchestva," in *Vtoraia proza: Russkaia proza 20-x–30-x godov XX veka*, ed. W. Weststeijn, D. Rizzi, and T. V. Tsiv'ian (Trent: Dipartimento di Scienze Filologiche e Storiche, 1995), 23–43. Memoirs include Marina Chukovskaia's "Odinochestvo" and

Veniamin Kaverin's "Dobychin," in *Pisatel' Leonid Dobychin: Vospominaniia, Stat'i, Pis'ma,* ed. Vladimir Bakhtin (St. Petersburg: AOZT "Zhurnal 'Zvezda,'" 1996), 7–15 and 16–19. See also Victor Erofeyev, "Nastoiashchii pisatel'," introduction to *Gorod En; Rasskazy,* by L. Dobychin (Moscow: Khudozhestvennaia literatura, 1989), 5–14; Richard C. Borden, "Introduction," in *The Town of N,* by Leonid Dobychin, trans. Borden with Natalia Belova (Evanston, Ill.: Northwestern University Press, 1998), vii–xxvi; and Richard C. Borden, "The Flogging Angel: Toward a Mapping of Leonid Dobychin's *Gorod En,*" *The Russian Review* 60, no. 2 (2001).

3. Simon Karlinsky, "Nabokov and Chekhov: The Lesser Russian Tradition," in *Nabokov: Criticism, Reminiscences, Translations, and Tributes,* ed. Alfred Appel Jr. and Charles Newman (Evanston, Ill.: Northwestern University Press, 1970), 7–16, uses this term to distinguish writers such as Chekhov and Nabokov, who valued art over ideology, from the more prominent tradition in Russian letters, the "humanitarian" literature of ideas and social commitment.

4. *Dobychin-99,* 247–328.

5. The Oberiu, the "Union of Real Art" or "Association of the Art of Reality" (*Ob"edinenie real'nogo iskusstva*), was a Leningrad-oriented group of avant-garde writers who banded together briefly, beginning in 1927, and included, most notably, Kharms, Alexander Vvedensky, Nikolai Zabolotsky, and Konstantin Vaginov. Formally experimental, the Oberiuty engaged in certain cubo-futurist practices, flirted with absurdism, and were the only Russian literary group that was close to surrealism.

6. In 1929 Kharms drew up plans for an anthology, to be entitled *Archimedes' Bath,* that was to have included works by Zabolotsky, Vvedensky, Kharms, Khlebnikov, Nikolai Tikhonov, Kaverin, Dobychin, Tynyanov, Shklovsky, and Olesha. See Anatolii Aleksandrov, "A Kharms Chronology," in *Daniil Kharms and the Poetics of the Absurd,* ed. Neil Cornwell (New York: St. Martin's Press, 1991), 38.

7. Solomon Volkov, for example, observes: "Dobychin's work was an extreme expression of the attempts by some masters of the new Petersburg prose to achieve simplicity and a laconic tone." Volkov also writes: "A writer who surpassed Zoshchenko in a desire for simplicity and laconic writing was Leonid Dobychin . . . Dobychin's works, which were greatly esteemed among Leningrad writers, were met with hostility by the critics

as collections of 'man-in-the-street gossip, foul anecdotes and operetta episodes.'" He goes on to cite a critic, who wrote: "The streets of Leningrad are filled with various people, most of whom are healthy, life-loving and energetic builders of socialism, but the author writes: 'Gnats bustled.'" Solomon Volkov, *St. Petersburg: A Cultural History*, trans. Antonina W. Bouis (New York: The Free Press, 1995), 383–84.

8. Tat'iana Nikol'skaia, "Vozvrashchenie talanta," in Bakhtin, *Pisatel' Leonid Dobychin*, 60.

9. N. Stepanov, *Zvezda* no. 11 (1927), 170, and O. Reznik, "Pozornaia kniga," *Literaturnaia gazeta* no. 10 (1931).

10. Among Russian emigrés, on the other hand, *The Town of N* received a rave review in the Paris newspaper *Poslednie novosti* by a leading writer and critic, Georgy Adamovich. Adamovich closes his encomium with the words: "What a strange, what a merciless and original thing. Remember the name of Dobychin: this might be a remarkable writer." Quoted in Roman Timenchik, "O gorode En, ego izobrazitele i o nes-byvshemsia prorochestve," in Bakhtin, *Pisatel' Leonid Dobychin*, 186.

11. "International Books of the Year," *Times Literary Supplement*, December 2, 1994.

12. Ibid.

13. Victor Erofeyev, "Russia's *Fleurs du Mal*," introduction to *The Penguin Book of New Russian Writing: Russia's Fleurs du Mal*, ed. Erofeyev and Andrew Reynolds (London and New York: Penguin, 1995), xiii.

14. The first English translation of *The Town of N* appeared in 1998 (see note 2). Slightly altered versions of "Ninon" and "The Sailor" (under the title "Lyoshka") appeared in *The Kenyon Review* (New Series) 23, no. 1 (Winter 2001), 29–35.

15. Aside from Joyce, Dobychin's detractors and admirers have linked his writing to numerous authors, notably Anton Chekhov, Andrei Bely, Nikolai Gogol, Marcel Proust, Fyodor Sologub, Bruno Schulz, Mikhail Saltykov-Shchedrin, Gustave Flaubert, Honoré de Balzac, Mikhail Bulgakov, and Ilya Ilf and Yevgeny Petrov. On the other hand, Veniamin Kaverin (*Epilog* [Moscow: Agraf, 1997], 209) sides with Dobychin's view of himself: " . . . he had no neighbors, no teachers, no pupils. He didn't recall anyone. He was by himself" (editor's translation).

Dobychin was repeatedly accused of modeling his novel *The Town of N* on Joyce's *Ulysses* (1922), which was widely discussed in the Soviet Union in the early and mid-1930s. Like Joyce, Dobychin writes about a real city, incorporating true-life events, places, and people, with their real names and all, in his fiction. Dobychin had conceived his novel, however, before *Ulysses* was well known in Russia. On the other hand, several articles about Joyce had appeared in Soviet journals in the early and mid-1920s, in at least one of which the scandalous reception of Joyce's reproduction of a real city and its inhabitants was discussed. V. S. Bakhtin suggests that this discussion might have led Dobychin to use an analogical conceit for his novel. Bakhtin also reports that *Dubliners* was published in Russian translation in Leningrad in 1927, and that Dobychin's editor for *The Town of N* at the publishing house Mysl' was the translator of parts of *Ulysses* into Russian. He concludes that Dobychin doubtless knew of Joyce and likely had read him. See Bakhtin, "Pod igom dobrykh nachal'nikov," in *Dobychin-99*, 37–42. There is no evidence, however, that Dobychin had read Joyce before 1927, when his distinctive story style was already developed.

16. This is a paraphrase of Joyce's own words regarding *Dubliners*. See *The Letters of James Joyce*, vol. 2, ed. Richard Ellmann (New York: Viking, 1966), 134.

17. A. Walton Litz makes this point regarding Joyce's *Dubliners* in *James Joyce* (Boston: Twayne, 1966), 50–51. I have used Litz's characterizations of *Dubliners* as part of my comparison.

18. Death by drowning figures so frequently in Dobychin's writing that one suspects he is parodying the high incidence of the "drowning" motif in Russian cultural history at large. This is certainly true in the case of the story "Encounters with Lise," for which Nikolai Karamzin's sentimental classic, *Poor Liza* (1792), provides a satirical subtext. V. N. Toporov reads "Encounters with Lise" as a comic-parodic updating of Karamzin's tale of romantic betrayal and drowning in "Rasskaz L. Dobychina *Vstrechi s Liz v kontekste Bednoi Lizy* 'Zheleznogo veka,'" in Weststeijn, Rizzi, and Tsiv'ian, *Vtoraia proza*, 77–111. In turn, "drowning" is a subset of a "water" theme that extends across Dobychin's oeuvre, as noted by Victor Erofeyev in "O Kukine i mirovoi garmonii," in Bakhtin, *Pisatel' Leonid Dobychin*, 51–56, and developed by Eduard Meksh in his articles in *Pisatel' Leonid Dobychin*.

19. Along with the cinematograph, parades, and corpses, themes and motifs that unite Dobychin's stories include: newspapers; "cavaliers" and

longing maidens; statues and monuments; perfumes and mirrors; body and facial hair; the conflict over nude bathing; water as the source of both life and death; and the matter of what people read.

Of this last theme, it is perhaps noteworthy that while in *The Town of N* Dobychin uses allusions to literary classics—the Bible, Gogol's *Dead Souls* (1842), Fyodor Dostoevsky's *The Idiot* (1868–69) and *A Raw Youth* (1875), Miguel de Cervantes's *Don Quixote* (1605, 1615), and Chekhov's "The Steppe" (1888)—as an important source of irony and for informing his characters' understanding of the world, in his stories he more often alludes to literary flops, such as James Fenimore Cooper's *Mercedes of Castile* (1840), Octave Mirbeau's *Torture Garden* (1899), and Upton Sinclair's *Jimmie Higgins* (1919), or the mediocre "classics" of Soviet socialist realism, such as Lidiya Seifullina's *Virineya* (1924).

20. This is Marvin Magalaner's and Richard M. Kain's paraphrase of Joyce's definition of an aesthetic "epiphany." See Magalaner and Kain, *Joyce* (New York: New York University Press, 1956), 70.

21. Irene Hendry, "Joyce's Epiphanies," in *James Joyce: Two Decades of Criticism*, ed. Seon Givens (New York: Vanguard, 1963), 30.

22. Joyce's stories are less minimalistic than Dobychin's. They are less shorn of description and retain a measure of lexical richness that Dobychin denies himself. Like Dobychin, however, Joyce never includes the merely ornamental; each detail is indispensable. The story in which Joyce's poetics approach Dobychin's most closely is "Ivy Day in the Committee Room" (1914).

23. In the case of "Old Ladies in a Small Town," which is set in pre-Soviet times, the political "parades"—both metaphorical and actual—manifest Russian imperial chauvinism.

24. Though its focus is *The Town of N*, a good introduction to Dobychin's poetics is Iurii Shcheglov, "*Zametki o proze Leonida Dobychina ('Gorod En'),*" *Literaturnoe obozrenie* 3, nos. 7/8, 25–36.

Encounters with Lise
and Other Stories

»»» «««

Farewell

Winter was drawing to a close. At six o'clock it was already light. Opening his eyes, Kunst would see the cracks on the ceiling, and from the cracks there would form a skirt and crooked legs wearing shoes with two little tabs. Behind the wall the nurse would already be shuffling her heelless shoes and waking the wounded man. Knocking at the door, the landlady would bring the kettle. "Disgraceful," she'd say, and point toward the wall with her head. Falling silent, she'd eavesdrop and then laugh. Kunst would redden.

Wearing his student coat, with a little piece of bread in his pocket, wrapped in the newspaper *The Age*, he would leave the house. The snow was dark. Buds like little horns stuck out at the ends of branches. Old women were returning from queue ranks and clasping bread to their jackets. Mad soldiers, dispersing from the field hospitals, muttered as they went. The laundress Kubarikha would meet and greet him. Respectable folk have scattered, she would grieve, there are no longer the same sort of lodgers. See, even she had taken in a nightbird, a pavement nymph.

A tram rang. "Move forward," the conductor exclaimed. The ice on the rivers had already gone gray. It was dry in front of houses. Saboteurs with newspapers were shouting on corners. On the other side of Trinity Bridge, Kunst climbed out and walked along the embankment. Dark palaces watched gloomily. Old stone men stood in faded red-brown niches, spreading their hands and executing a pas.

Ivan Ilyich would already be writing, frail, at the big desk with the mother-of-pearl birds, and Mirra Osipovna, tidying her hair, would already be seated. Wearing a fur collar, she would huddle up and tremble now and then. "Listen, I'm freezing," she'd say languidly as she draped herself.

Chief Glan, short, wearing a short suit, would arrive at a run and, settling down in the armchair, unfold his newspaper, *The Beam.* "'Facing Hunger!'" he'd peruse loudly. The girl Malanya, swaying her fleshy parts, would hand out tea. The men would take side glances at her. Instructor Baumshtein would drop by with a report, and Chief Glan would listen to him majestically. "At your service," Instructor Baumshtein would salute and wink at the maidens. "But is he ever attractive," they'd marvel. "I'm writing a master's thesis," Ivan Ilyich would then say, glancing at the windows, "and every evening for several hours I forget this life." "Ah, I understand you," Mirra Osipovna would say, dropping her head to one side and smiling tenderly.

"Time," at last, tearing himself away, Chief Glan would fold up his *Beam.* Everyone would leap into action. Powder and pencils for the lips were taken out. Ivan Ilyich would look at himself in the desk's lacquer and, with a modest air, freshen the parting in his hair. Standing by the exit would be saboteurs with newspapers. "The Eeeveneeeng," they'd yell ringingly and hop up and down. Squat generals with the *New Times* would slap their hands against their sides and stamp their feet. The fortress spire glittered. Sea clouds flew.

Throwing off his shoes and taking *The Age* in his hands, Kunst
would cautiously, so as not to rumple his trousers, lie down on the
bed. The nurse would be snoring softly behind the wall. Frieda
would return from the office and make a stir. Knocking at the door,
the landlady would bring in the kettle. "What's in the papers?"
she'd ask, and take a seat. "Frieda keeps on singing. She's so poetical. I was different." Sometimes, tittering mysteriously, she'd make
a playful face. "A letter," she'd say, handing it over with grimaces
and slyly laughing. "Probably from some pretty little thing."
Kunst would take the envelope and, looking at the light, unseal it.
Auntie was writing. "Come," she'd invite him. "We eat our fill.
And you have such horrors. Recently I was reading that a certain
professor swelled up from hunger and a writer lady collapsed in a
dead faint."

The snow melted. It dried out a bit. The ice passed—together
with its roads and ski tracks. Peasant women with willow branches
sat down in the streets. "We're going to get a distribution,"
announced Ivan Ilyich, adjusting his little jacket and rubbing his
hands. "Honey with bees," Mirra Osipovna said as she leapt up
and, counting, bent back a finger. Her collar flew open; a "dancing
woman" brooch was revealed. "Red caviar and stewed pears in
tins!" Toward the end of the day a bony maiden with a yellow head
tore across the room. "Don't go away," she announced. "Wait. I'll
go for the distribution in the truck." "Take two armed men," they
shouted to her. "I will," she said, turning, and brightly casting a
glance. "And I'll arm myself." "The maiden Simon," said Ivan
Ilyich. Seeing her off with his eyes, he looked around. "Perhaps
Simòn would be more correct," he conjectured later, having
thought a bit. They waited a long time. The electricity wasn't
functioning. The girl Malanya brought a lantern and had a little

chuckle. "Like watering cows," she compared. Shadows appeared. Outside the window, the news sellers were shouting in singsong voices, "Eee-ve-neeeng." Kunst, leaning against the windowsill, softly took part in their song, and Ivan Ilyich, timidly, joined him.

Tears were streaming
from the station

they sang together in a whisper, feeling embarrassed.

Easter had arrived. There was nothing to do. Kunst slept, looked at himself in the mirror, ate his distribution. The landlady would open the door, thrust her head through, and ask whether it smelled of fumes. "Ah, look what you got," she examined closely and clasped her hands to her heart. "Frieda got *vobla:* also good." In the next room the nurse was entertaining her colleagues. They were beating a tambourine, drinking spirits, and quacking. They cursed the wounded: "You barely go out," they said, "and already he's rummaging through your basket." The smell of disinfectant wafted from them. Frieda, poetical, let down her hair, opened the ventilation window in the corridor, and sang. The madmen, listening spellbound, stood before the front garden. Kunst went out, and they set off after him. He met Kubarikha wearing holiday apparel. "Do drop in," she pressed, and served Easter cake with a flower on the upper crust and eggs. The nightbird—the pavement nymph—had been invited. Prettily curled, she coughed modestly, in order to clear her throat, and courteously said, "Yes, please," and "No, merci." "There, that's right," Kubarikha encouraged her, and she would redden.

Moving aside last year's leaves, blades of grass were starting to climb up out of the earth. A little bird appeared on the Black River, and in the evenings it would softly whistle from time to time. The nightbird took to walking beneath the windows. Embarrassed, Kunst would draw the curtain. Refugees from Riga began arriving from the city on Sundays. Removing their stockings and shoes, they would sit by the water. The landlady would don a lace kerchief and go out to take a look at them. "My compatriots," she would explain.

Mirra Osipovna stopped freezing and removed her collar. She carried branches with little leaves with her and, requesting a mug from the girl Malanya, would put them in water. Instructor Baumshtein would come running in and, stooped over, sniff them. "Ah," lifting up his eyes, he'd sigh. "The year's morn," Ivan Ilyich would say, adjusting his clothing. The mother-of-pearl on his desk glittered. Outside the window, the sky shone a dark blue. Kunst was lost in contemplation, and he recalled the letter from Auntie.

Opening the door halfway one day, the maiden Simon shouted that bonuses had been ordered. "Is it possible?" Mirra Osipovna doubted languidly as she arose. The girl Malanya appeared amid the uproar. "Come get them," she invited, baring her teeth. Everybody dashed. "Sign for them," the bookkeeper exulted behind the table and cut the sheets of money. "An efficient little lady," they said of her, clustering around. "A lesson for skeptics," Ivan Ilyich said, and looked at Mirra Osipovna. The girl Malanya smacked someone on the hands. It was pleasant. A day later a man arrived and convened a meeting: the union does not permit bonuses. It was decreed that they'd have to be deducted, and they returned to their places dejected. "Not what I was expecting," Mirra Osipovna said gloomily. Pulling her branch with leaves from the mug, she broke it. "Have you read Max Stirner?" Ivan Ilyich asked as he wandered about, bent over and nose hanging. Kunst was thinking, laying his head on his arms.

7

"I'm coming," he wrote to Auntie, and then bought a ticket. The landlady brought the evening kettle for the last time. "I'd leave myself," she said as she sat down and rubbed her eyes with her sleeve. "Courland Province," she said solemnly, shaking her head from time to time. "I'll never forget you." Kunst went out onto the porch. A lusterless moon, red, ponderous, like a marmalade crescent, stole over the backyards. Muffled up in a big shawl, the nurse, motionless, was sitting on a stair. Kunst sat down above. The red west was lined with dusty streaks. Far away a locomotive whistled. "Filyanka," whispered the nurse, not stirring. "Perhaps the seaside," thought Kunst silently. With the dawn a cabbie rolled up. Rain trickled. "Farewell," cried the landlady from the porch. "Farewell," Kunst turned. "Farewell," Frieda leaned out of the window, "farewell." Poetical, in a blanket and cap, she waved her naked arms. The nightbird—the pavement nymph— yawning from time to time, was walking home. "Farewell."

Kozlova

1

Electricity burned in the three church chandeliers. Forty-eight
Soviet office workers were singing in the choir. The newly arrived
preacher prophesied that soon God would rise again and his enemies would be scattered.

Kozlova kissed the icon and, rubbing the oil on her forehead,
jostled her way through to the exit. She barely squeezed her way
across the square: they were setting off rockets, shoving one
another, yelling something, burning a cardboard God the Father
with his head in a triangle, music was playing "The International."

"Scoundrels," whispered Kozlova, "persecutors . . ." Snow
crunched underfoot. The places oiled by sledge runners shone
greasily. Over the Karl Liebknecht and Rosa Luxemburg School
stood a little greenish moon. Kozlova sighed: here Monsieur Poincaré had taught French.

She slowed. Pleasant pictures of friendship with Monsieur
arose in memory.

Here is—tea.

Monsieur is telling about Our Lady of Lourdes. Avdotya
opens the door and spies. Kozlova points to her with her eyes.
"Affable woman," says Monsieur. Then he takes up his hat,
Kozlova rises, and they are reflected in the mirror: he—tidy,
gray, taking his leave; she—erect, wearing a long dress, fingers

of the left hand in fingers of the right, a refined nose slightly aslant, on tight lips, an old-fashioned smile. "Do come again, Monsieur . . ."

And here they are—at the cinematograph. A violin is playing. Monsieur is leaving tomorrow. Leaves fall slowly from a slender little tree in a green tub. "How sad, Monsieur . . ." A maiden in a red knit jacket draws back the curtain and admits them. Along the sides of the canvas hang Lenin and Trotsky . . . A comical mother-in-law smashes crockery and breaks furniture, Swiss lakes show off their beauty, and six portions of a sumptuous drama are glimpsed fleetingly: Clotilda poisoned herself, Janna threw herself from a window, and Charles slowly sailed away on the steamship *Republic*, and it begins to seem to him that everything that had happened was but a dream.

"And so too will you, Monsieur, forget us, like a dream."

"Oh, Mademoiselle!"

The return voyage is replete with effusions. In beautiful France Monsieur will think of her. He will keep up with politics.

"But whomsoever could one call the Sibyl of our times, if not Madame de Thèbes," he will write, when something of the sort could be expected . . .

2

Kozlova sat through her evenings on the stove bench, darning linen or reading the supplement to *The Cornfield*. Tuesday was women's day: she would go with Avdotya to the baths, where children bawled, washbasins rattled, fat-paunched peasant women with their hair let down, steaming, lashed themselves with birch twigs. On Sunday they'd each take a basket and set off for the market. "Citizen, dear citizen," the market women pressed, thrusting themselves out of the stalls. "Lady dear!" or "Little miss!"

Sometimes Suslova would come over, and they'd drink tea for a long time: the hostess—decorous, with a courteous smile; the guest—disheveled, fat, with elbows on the table and noisy sighs. They'd talk of the difficult life and of olden times. Avdotya would listen, standing in the doorway.

"In Petersburg I saw someone," the round-cheeked Suslova would relate, staring pensively at the teacups (one had on it the Winter Palace, the other, the Admiralty). "Don't know, maybe the Empress herself. I'm walking past the palace, suddenly a carriage drives up, out jumps a lady and flies up the porch."

"Perhaps the housekeeper with the shopping," Kozlova would answer . . .

Winter passed. On the first of May, Kozlova laundered two jackets and a half-dozen shawls: let them choke on that. Through the open windows flew the sounds of orchestras . . . The icon of Saint Kuksha had been brought from the monastery. They went to meet it. Returned agitated.

"Scoundrels, persecutors . . ."

"Good Lord, when will we be spared them? . . . Does Moussiour not write?"

Later the moon rose, and their spirits eased . . . A peal was rung in the cathedral. A waltz played in "Red October" Park. They encountered Demeshchenko, Garashchenko, and Kalegaeva, pensive, with bird cherry twigs.

They stopped above the river and looked awhile at the moon's stripe and a boat with a balalaika.

"Venezia," whispered Kozlova.

"*Venezia e Napoli*," Suslova answered. Falling silent for a while, softly and dreamily she said, "When the cooperative store was on fire, the perfumes began to burn, and it smelled so good . . ."

Toward morning someone coughed by the bed. Kozlova turned and saw Saint Kuksha, wearing a dark blue ecclesiastical stole, as on the icon. He handed her a charter, and she read what had been written there: "But whomsoever could one call the Sibyl of our times, if not Madame de Thèbes."

She awoke agitated and left a bit earlier in order to stop by the cathedral before going to the office. The door was locked. Kozlova jogged the gate and sat down to wait in the garden.

A column with a transfiguration and a green dome stood over the maples. Loose flesh-colored clouds were melting away, and a blue glimmered through them in places. A door creaked, the bishop came out of the lodge—bareheaded, with a bucket of slops. He stood awhile, counting the strokes of the clock on the watch-tower, and turned over his bucket beneath the column with the transfiguration.

"Won't be tormented long," thought Kozlova joyfully, following him with her eyes.

She ate dinner hastily—wanted to see Suslova, but, rising from the table, grew languid and barely made it to bed. Upon awaking she felt too lazy to go to Suslova's. Dispatched Avdotya to meet the cow and went into the vegetable garden. The sun was setting, and the sunset was unpretentious: one little stripe reddish and one greenish. Kozlova was a lover of watering. "When you're watering," she would say, "the soul rests and sinks into a sweet state."

She was pouring the twelfth watering can and the moon was glittering in the rapidly disappearing little puddles. An orchestra began to thunder, and Kozlova rushed to the gates.

Sneezed from the dust. Smoky fires fluttered on torches and reflected in the copper trumpets. Curzon dangled on the gallows. Light flitted across the marchers' faces.

"Hut, two! Left! Long live the Communist Party! Hurrah!"

Gaping, Suslova was marching.

Avdotya came running from out of the darkness. "England's joined the war."

They illuminated the little lights before the icon cases and, by the brightness of two lamps, drank real tea. It reeked of kerosene and soot.

With a radiant face, Kozlova got a little jar of raspberries from the medicine cabinet. "Easter," Avdotya delighted. That fool Suslova was roundly abused.

3

They were sitting doing overtime. Flies were biting. A big bell droned, and, tinkling, the windowpanes joined in.

Demeshchenko had bent over the table and was scratching out "Comrade Lenin."

Garashchenko and Kalegaeva, lounging on chairs, were gnawing sunflower seeds and gawking at the new one.

"Tomorrow's John the Warrior," said the new one, a fussy old lady with red cheeks. "Whenever you quarrel with someone, pray to John the Warrior. I always do, and, you know, she was taken away and sentenced to three years."

"A good woman," thought Kozlova, "religious . . . Sutyrkina, I think."

She passed her papers and inkpot to Sutyrkina. "Where do you live?"

They left together: Kozlova—staid, wearing a dark blue gauze scarf with indistinct yellow circles; Sutyrkina—fidgety, wearing an old straw hat with feathers.

By gates cavaliers were putting on airs before maidens. Little boys were bawling, "Boldly to battle we shall go." The dust raised during the day was settling. The debris of trees planted on "Tree Day" was sticking up. Carrion wafted.

"My canvas coat," Sutyrkina was saying, "I received from the *finkotrud* union. In the year nineteen I guarded their garden, lived in a straw hut. Acquaintances would come by, and, I'll tell you, without boasting, we spent evenings full of poetry."

Kozlova listened with an expression such as though she had candy in her mouth: evenings full of poetry!

"You say, in the year nineteen," she said in an amiable and pleasing voice. "Remember, everyone then would sigh—I'd like to eat this, like to eat that. But I had one dream: to have a drink of good coffee with a little Easter cake."

They became friends. Often they would drink tea at each other's place and, when there was no rain, take a stroll out of town. They'd converse about their superiors, about the regeneration of icons, about former vogues.

"You didn't happen to be at the provincial olympiad?" Sutyrkina would sometimes ask. "Almost completely naked! Ugh, what indecency." And, smiling, for a long time would remain silent and gaze into the distance.

Once or twice they encountered Suslova, and she would stop and, turning, look at them until they'd disappeared from view . . .

Sun glittered in the looking-glass crosses. Maples shone brightly yellow. The rowan trees with their red clusters reminded Kozlova of little bouquets of wild strawberries. She stopped, inclined her head to one side, and, holding her left hand in her right, picturesquely admired them.

Sutyrkina caught up with her. "Not bad weather. I'd go to the exhibition with pleasure. Very pretty, it's said, Lenin made of flowers." Kozlova pursed her lips.

"You know," Sutyrkina said to her with dignity, "I always take into consideration the spirit of the times. Right now the spirit is such that one goes to the exhibition, to supplement one's agricultural knowledge . . ."

» «

Rain tapped against the glass. Black twigs rocked outside the windows. It was dark in the office. Demeshchenko, Garashenko, and Kalegaeva yawned and stood for a long time by the stove. Sutyrkina was reading the newspaper.

"Here are two interesting announcements."

Everybody looked at her, and she rose and cleared her throat. One was from Kharin: on November 7 he has an enormous assortment of bread and confectionery wares. The other was from the bishop: on November 7 there will be a ceremonial mass and a thanksgiving service in all churches.

"Understand what the spirit is now?"

4

Kozlova was sitting on the warm stove bench reading the supplement to *The Cornfield*. Avdotya was sweeping the floor. It smelled of mice from the supplement and of wormwood from the wormwood whisk. Alexandra Nikolaevna got wedded to Pyotr Ivanovich; standing at the altar, they shone with beauty. But Alexei Yegorich would visit them every holiday and, sitting in the comfortable armchair after a substantial dinner, would heave a deep sigh from time to time.

Kozlova shut her eyes and enjoyed that pleasant ending for a few minutes. Then she took four pins from a little wooden box with lilac-colored violets and pinned up a skirt. She had painted those violets herself when she was young . . .

She put on her felt boots, a knitted cap, and a jacket and went to take a stroll.

Suslova came running up: red, wearing a large shawl, with a rooster under her arm.

"So, how's it going?" she muttered. "Long time since we've met . . . Life is hard. Here, I bought a rooster—for two meals. In such a family . . . Does Moussiour not write?"

Kozlova took her by the hands. "Come by at half past five."

Bright-eyed jackdaws hopped along the road. Storm clouds hung low. Sometimes snowflakes flew past.

Chuckling at pleasant thoughts, Kozlova wandered the streets. Turned in at the cemetery with headstones that resembled washbasins and, smiling, bowed to her parents' graves.

The Saint Kuksha Monastery was visible from the gates—little slender churches, potbellied turrets. It came back to her: the red-brown palace, the yellow Admiralty . . .

This evening the sensitive Suslova will stare at the teacups, grow quiet, become pensive and tell about how she'd seen the Empress. Cozy, like in the novel from the supplement, the samovar will make a noise, the lamp will snugly smell faintly of kerosene. "You, it seems, encountered me with that woman," Kozlova will say. "She and I did not have a genuine friendship."

Electricity lit up on the poles—little yellow specks beneath the gray storm clouds. Two cartloads of firewood entered the gates of the Karl Liebknecht and Rosa Luxemburg School . . . Here had taught Monsieur Poincaré.

» » »   « « «

Encounters with Lise

1

Wriggling her shoulders as she went, head lifted high, with a triumphant smile on her face, violet with powder, Lise Kuritsyna turned off German Revolution Street onto Third International Street.

Turning her torso right, then left, with each step, she swung, like a censer, a braided string bag into which had been squeezed a blue basin with yellow flowers.

Kukin turned across his left shoulder and walked smartly behind her as far as the bathhouse. There she stopped, turned, triumphantly glanced right and left, and flew up onto the porch.

The door banged. Market women, sitting on pots filled with hot coals, offered Kukin pickled apples. Not looking at them, joyful, he descended to the river.

"Perhaps," he dreamed, "she's already taken off her clothes. Oh, to hell with it!"

An icy crust on the snow sparkled in the evening sun. Driving horses, peasant men came riding from the bazaar. Files of peasant women walked with bunches of unsold bast shoes and lay down on their paunches at an ice hole and, lowering their heads, sucked up the water.

"Animals," Kukin gloated.

When he was walking back through the orchard, the moon was high, and beneath the entangled branches of apple trees slender shadows lay upon the snow.

"In three months it will be white with fallen petals here," thought Kukin, and he pictured to himself thrilling scenes between him and Lise, settled upon the white petals.

He had a laugh at the pranks of the young people who were beckoning cabbies and then saying, "Drive on by," and in a pleasant mood he turned into his lane.

The penal battalion club was illumined festively, music rumbled within, and on a door decorated with fir branches hung an announcement: the battalion troupe presents two plays, "When Mother-in-Law's a Guest, All's an Awful Mess" and an antireligious one.

The teapot was already on the samovar. Mother was sitting with the Gospels.

"I've been to confession."

Kukin made a pious face, and to the ticking of the "*Le roi à Paris*" clock began drinking cup after cup—the gray-haired mother in a calico dress and her son in a sailcloth shirt with a little black tie, lanky, gaunt, with a hedgehog haircut.

2

Into the office hobbled lame Riva Golubushkina and gave the order to go see Fishkina—to rule paper.

"Read the newspaper?" she asked, lifting her brows. "There's an article by Fishkina: 'Don't abuse portraits of the leaders.'" And, throwing back her head, she rolled out her bosoms.

It was cold. A wet wind blew through the open window.

Riva was diligently rewriting. Kukin, standing, was ruling.

Fishkina, bringing her dark face nearer his arm, watched, and her black hairdo touched his colorless hair. Then she roused herself and moved away to the window.

She stood, short, dark, erect, and disdainful, peering at the storm clouds. Then she softly blew her nose and, turning toward the room, said, "Comrade Kukin."

The door opened slightly, and someone peeped in. She put on a yellow calfskin jacket and left.

"She liked you," Riva congratulated, rolling out her bosoms and mysteriously looking around. "Try to get in good with her: she'll promote you. It's only a shame they're transferring her and me. But never mind, I'll be arranging some meetings for you."

"It's possible," Kukin rejoiced. "After all, I'm not against the lowest classes. I'm prepared to sympathize." And, exulting, he whistled, "Rise, accursed."

Red and blue balloons rushed about on the wind above a bearded hawker. Cripples wailed on corners. From house to house went an old woman in a black jacket:

> For Christ's sake, give alms
> To a deaf, sick old lady—
> By your largesse
> Be our benefactress.

By a gate with four green tin-plate vases that had fallen in various directions, Kukin put his hand on his heart: here lives Lise, languishing in compresses. She has boils on her back—her letter headed "Our Bathhouses" had been printed in the newspaper.

In the library hung placards: "Tuberculosis! The working people's disease!"; "Down with Household Breeding Grounds!"

"Anything revolutionary," requested Kukin.

The girl with yellow ringlets hopped off and up the little ladders.

"Not at present. Take something else. *Mercedes of Castile,* the works of Pisemsky . . ."

Oh, to hell with it—he had already been seeing himself with those books, encountering Fishkina. "What's that you have? Really? So, then you sympathize!"

Mother was sitting on the divan with a guest—Zolotukhina, sinewy, wearing a guipure collar, pinned on with a silver rose.

"Haven't heard of any impending change of regime, have you?" asked Zolotukhina languidly, holding out her hand.

"Change is not expected," Kukin answered severely. "And you know, many were against, but now, on the contrary, sympathize."

Done with civilities, the old ladies continued their conversation.

"Where is spring so pretty," sighed Zolotukhina, "as it is in Petersburg? The snow hasn't melted yet, but already they're selling flowers on the sidewalks. I used to dress at de Notkina's. 'Fashions by de Notkina' . . .

"Well, and you, young man: Do you remember the capital? Student days? It is, after all, the very best time, gay . . ."

She narrowed her eyes and turned her head.

"I'll say," said Kukin. "Cultural life . . ." And he felt pleasantly sad and fell into a reverie over his soup: a music box plays, the students have grown pensive, take their beer with salted soaked peas . . .

Oh, Petersburg!

3

"Let's go, let's go," called Zolotukhina. "Down with Rumania."

Kukina was refusing, showing her holey soles . . .

They walked for a long time. Flags fluttered up and, subsiding, brushed against one's nose.

Eh, you, bourgeoisie,
Eh, you, smart alecks.

The moon shone a vague white speck. Sky showed through the bell towers' quadrangular apertures. Tree tops with swollen buds stirred.

"Well, everything will fall to pieces," sighed Kukina, shaking her head at the little houses, slanting and propped up with logs. "Where to live then?"

Fishkina looked disdainfully right and left. "Ugh, how much philistinism!"

Hobbling in front, Riva looked around at Kukin and nodded and, shrugging her shoulders, turned away; he hadn't seen her. In front of him, waving her arms to the music, Lise was marching and swiveling the small of her back. When the trumpets stopped, Kukin heard her chirping with her neighbor:

"People are admitted into the *gubsoyuz* solely through patronage . . ."

Into the office came a boy.

"Don't lose time," Riva had dispatched a note and a ticket to the Karl Marx and Friedrich Engels Garden. "Try to get in good with Fishkina. She'll promote you. Have you read *The Torture Garden?*—a magical thing."

"Lise," said Kukin, "I'll be true to you . . ."

"My feet have gone bad," complained Mother. "I made meat jelly and fritters, wanted to take them to the monsignor, but, really, I can't. I'll ask Granny Alexandrikha, and you be so kind, Georges, as to keep an eye on her from a distance."

"Just a minute," said Kukin and, reaching the end of "*Blancmange*," shut the book, interleaved with ribbons and dried flowers.

"Ah," he sighed, "the old days won't be coming back."

The penals, creeping in a squatting position, painstakingly wrote out with little bricks on a strip alongside the battalion, spread with sand, "Proletariat of all nations, unite!"

Lise, violet, with a violet umbrella, with a yellow ribbon in hair dyed with hydrogen peroxide, watched.

Kukin stopped and was adjusting his shirt. Lise began to laugh, swayed, tore herself from the spot, and set off.

Should follow her—but it was impossible to leave Alexandrikha without supervision.

They returned together—Alexandrikha in a sackcloth vest and striped apron and the dejected Kukin in the sailcloth shirt with the little black tie—and as a whitish reflection they could be glimpsed fleetingly in the little black windows.

"In the morning the spirit tends to be very free," Alexandrikha recounted . . .

Little boys and girls were running. Proprietresses came out to meet the cows. The sunset's redness was reflected in the gloss of benches.

It began to smell of powder: on the porch of Saint Euplus a wedding thronged. What an omen!

4

In the water vaguely, like a landscape on a divan pillow, a hill with churches shone green.

The sun scorched the backs and stomachs exposed to it.

"Working people of all nations," the cashier from the station was telling Kukin dreamily, "await their emancipation. Take a look, please, has it gotten red enough between my shoulder blades?"

Shurka Gusev, wet, panting, eyes shining, ran up along the shore and grabbed his trousers:

"Some girl drowned."

Peasant men, leaving their cartloads of firewood on the road; peasant women, in heavy cloth coats and pink skirts, with heaps of bast shoes on their backs; and bathers, doing up buttons, all thronged.

"Here are her clothes," Riva Golubushkina's mother, rotund, wearing a straight black wig with a parting, mysteriously pointed. "You know her wont: to twirl her tail before the men. She had swum out beyond the bend so the men would see . . ."

"Why aren't you getting in good with her?" wrote Riva. "I'll send a ticket again. Make sure you do it. There's a vocal number:

> He who's got funds,
> Can always come back,
> But he who got none— ·
> Can peep through a crack."

"After it go up to her at once and say: 'What utter philistinism! I am astonished; no Marxist approach whatsoever!'"

A dusty beam made its way through the shutters. They were eating *kisel'* and, sweaty, waving, cursing the flies. The sound of a little bell, the sound of a big one, softly flew in: at Saint Euplus they'd begun ringing for a funeral. They rushed to the windows, threw the flower pots to the floor, removed the shutters.

"Kuritsyna," announced Zolotukhina, leaning outside up to her waist.

Kukina crossed herself and caught hold of her nose. "Phew!"

"What do you want in this scorching heat," Zolotukhina said, standing up for her. "As for me, I'm sincerely sorry for her."

"Of course," said Kukin, "a girl with an education . . ."

After tea they went out onto the porch. The penals were singing "The International."

The silver rose on the guipure collar flashed. "In the companies," Zolotukhina roused herself, "the soldiers sing 'Our Father' and 'God, Tsar' at this hour. And in front of the barracks—little flower beds, pansies . . . I love this church," she pointed at yellow Euplus with its white pillars, "it recalls Petersburg."

Everyone turned their heads. Along the street, disdainfully casting glances, dark, sturdy, wearing a short tussah skirt and a blue jacket with white stripes, walked Fishkina.

"An interesting personage," said Kukina.

Georges straightened his little tie.

Lidiya

1

On her arm hung the basket with the purchases. Zaitseva extracted the "Voyage" eau de cologne and admired the little picture: travelers riding in a sleigh. She sniffed at it. With her right hand she brought the fifteen kopecks of ice cream toward her lips with their little white mustaches.

>Stream on,
>my pioneer song.

A thickset fellow with rolled-up sleeves, with fluff on his cheeks, paced to one side and, watching the marchers' legs, shouted importantly, "Left hup!"

"Whoever is that?" asked Zaitseva.

"Youth Leader," squeaked a towheaded girl holding a pillow-case who, casting a glance at Zaitseva, stretched the pillowslip over her head and hopped off into the wind.

By the locked gate Petka waited.

"Hello," he said. "A soldier drowned."

They took seats at the table beneath the pear tree. Petka did his homework. Zaitseva absentmindedly looked across the fence.

Clouds shone white in capricious figures. On the hillock, resembling an armored car, stood the squat gray Assumption with its flat cupola.

"Paradise was a beautiful garden in the East."

A beautiful garden! . . .

After dinner the husband read the paper. "Oh, those Chinese," he admired. He drank some tea and lay down to sleep. Dudkina, wearing a dark blue dress, arrived. They sat beneath the pear tree. The nanny goat began bleating by the gates.

They perked up. Scratched a bit between her horns, and she, content, half closed her yellow eyes with their white lashes.

"Took her to a billy goat?" asked Dudkina, interested.

The Assumption turned black against the colorless bright sky. The moon sailed into view.

"I've been trying all the liqueurs," Dudkina said pensively, "at Seleznyov's, at his dinners for teachers."

2

Zaitseva, wearing a prim dress with little blue posies, was sticking her elbows out so that the wind would freshen her sweated flanks. Short Dudkina could scarcely keep pace. The husband was panting from behind.

Svistunikha, wearing a little white kerchief, sprang out from the gate. Watched the road.

"I'm receiving the icon," she boasted.

"And we're off to the drowned man," yelled the husband.

They stopped by the cinematograph: Denikin atrocities had been posted. The heads of the buried were sticking up out of the ground. A girl was being bound to a tree . . .

In front of the shelter, shrieking over a game of cards, sat the defectives. "Zuev's house," sighed Dudkina. "There used to be a croquet court here. A tobacco plant would blossom . . ."

They passed the barracks, red, with yellow about the windows. Arm in arm, soldiers strolled about in twos and threes.

Spectators gadded about over the whirlpool. A guitar was being played. The sentry yawned.

The Zaitsevs poked awhile at the hummock, to see whether there were any ants. The husband unwrapped the food.

Young people in gold skullcaps, unfastening buttons, leapt down toward the river.

"Dive," they amused themselves, "and say 'under a bench.'"

They laughed, "While you were diving, we asked about where you'd been made."

Dudkina squinted. The husband snapped his fingers. "Eh, youth!"

"Left hup!" Zaitseva fell into a reverie.

Returning, they jabbered about politics.

"Should be driven from every quarter," the husband seethed.

"No, I'm—for educated nations," Dudkina disagreed.

They came upon Svistunikha. She had finished with the icon and was hurrying, while it was still light, to the drowned man.

3

The husband arrived, brows knitted. From the office he'd gone to bathe, and in a little lane on a fence he'd seen a shred of black placard with a yellow bowl: "Vote for the SR Party." He'd recollected the past, had been deeply moved . . . After dinner he cheered up.

"The drowned man," he recounted the news, "surfaced."

Zaitseva bought some snap fasteners. The little fountain gushed, and squat begonias and geraniums shone red before the statue of Comrade Figatner.

It grew dark. A branch broke off a tree. Dust flew.

"Snack Bar with All Cold Snacks," Zaitseva read over the door and leapt up.

"I was washing my hair," said the corpulent proprietress, smiling dejectedly, with her hair down. She uncorked *kvass.* "The stove repairer's over my place. Yesterday I put in a *drachyona*—and it came out completely hard."

On the table there was the palm of a hand with cigarette stubs. Two stemless roses floated in a saucer.

A wet maiden came running in, and, casting a sidelong glance inside the room, with stout fingers tore from her breasts the blouse that had stuck there.

"A rainbow!" the maiden sprang out. Zaitseva went out onto the front stoop with the proprietress.

The Youth Leader, thickset, without any belt, barefoot, brandishing a switch, was dispatching a billy goat out onto the street.

"Theirs?" beamed Zaitseva.

A storm cloud was running away. Sparrows screamed. Boys poured out onto the road, marching.

> The Red Army's the strongest
> of them all.

Cows trudged along. Pompous and white, swinging her round flanks and cocking a short leather-lined tail, came the nanny goat. Zaitseva was calling, "Lidiya, Lidiya!"

"Lidiya, Lidiya," the defectives called as they hung out from their windows.

The sunset shone on the signboard with the four hats. A waltz played. In the window of the little shop hung a haversack.

"Georgie!" Svistunikha began yelling, and came to a halt with buckets in her hands.

It's Lidiya who used to be called Georgie; Zaitseva had renamed her. "Not a woman's name," she would explain.

Savkina

1

Savkina, round cheeks shaking, peered at a paper written all over in red ink and poked her finger at the letters of the typewriter.

Air gusted. "Doors! Doors!" the clerks shouted. A cavalier entered—puny, curly-headed, fair . . .

The sun warmed the back of one's head. Wagons rattled. Conceited rich dames Frumkina and Fradkina strolled. Morkovnikova, shaded by bottles, watched from her kiosk. Trumpets sparkling, a funeral march played. Wreaths of pine branches and black flags were being carried. In a red coffin carted upon a curtained hearse was Olympia Kukel.

Savkina smoothed her sides with her palms and, taking a place in the ranks, marched several blocks. Sighed for a while. How recently it had been that they'd sat behind the sheds. The day had been drawing to its end. Midges jostled. "Everyone's dressed so properly there," Olympia assured and gaped. "Some have roses pinned . . . Ah, motherland, motherland! . . ."

The mother, red, stood at the cooker. Pavlushenka, stooped over a basin, was washing his hands: his short shirt, pulled back, was sticking out from under his belt, like the tail of a hare.

The table was laid. "Don't go too heavy on the pies," the mother warned and fell sorrowful. "Poor Olympia. No peals, no service . . ."

Done with the dishes, Savkina powdered herself, took a notebook, and, rubbing glycerin into her hands, went out behind the sheds to read verse. Kukel, wearing a dark blue apron, was milking a cow.

"They's offenderd there wasn't a priest," he complained. "And me being Party."

On the cover of the notebook was Gogol with little black mustaches.

"The Dnieper is lovely in calm weather."

A little white star appeared. Savkina, dreamy, rose and went toward the gates. The wake guests at Kukel's were raising a racket. Somewhere a trumpet softly played. Pavlushenka, with face grown pale and wet hair, returned from bathing. Gnawing on sunflower seeds, Kolya Yevreinov arrived. The collar of his short white and blue shirt was unbuttoned, and his black cloth trousers widened from the knees and at the bottom were like skirts.

2

Quadrangles of sun lay upon the floor with the shadows of ficus leaves and the light shadows of lace curtains. Savkina was brewing tea. Pavlushenka was shaving.

The mother, wearing a brown housecoat with little yellow flowers, was combing her hair.

"You should stop in, Nyushenka, at their church," she said, "and light a candle."

It was dark and cold in the little log church. The candle box was missing. The squat priest Valyukenas made a final curtsy before the altar and went off behind the screen. Sighing, Marya Ivanovna Babkina, the Frenchwoman, rose and walked past Savkina—wearing a straw hat with yellow satin, a striped jacket, and a black skirt with a yoke, trimmed with ribbons.

It reeked of burning. Litter rustled along the cobblestones. In the office hung a portrait of Mikhailova, who had won a hundred thousand. It stank of tobacco and something sour. The wall newspaper *Red Beam* was raking Comrade Samokhvalova over the coals: it turns out her uncle had had a shop . . .

Looking each other over, they paced the hall. In passing they would glance in the mirror. Savkina, wearing a lilac blouse like a bubble, was laughing, and her eyes darted through the crowd. Kolya Yevreinov bowed his shaved head to her. His collar was unfastened; under his clavicles little hairs shone black.

"Dressed like a bourgeois," he pointed. "Oh, the hell with her! . . ." On the picturesque riverbanks clustered villas. The steamships had passed each other by: Miss May and clubman Baybl had been standing on their decks . . . And now everything had become loathsome to Miss May. Advantageous proposals were not making her happy. Life wasn't amusing her. At times she would recline her head and reach out her hands toward the steamship that was sailing past in her dreams. Suddenly from out of an automobile sprang Baybl—in a hunting suit and Tyrolean hat.

Savkina was agitated. As though she had been shown her destiny . . .

Dogs barked. Dew dripped. In her kiosk, illumined by a candle, Morkovnikova dozed.

3

After dinner Savkina dreamed about the cavalier. She couldn't make out the face, but Savkina recognized him. He was wandering pensively among the graves and twirled a little hat in his hands.

The windows of the wing had been opened wide and splashed with whitewash: Kukel had moved to Zaretskaya, to a new wife. Apples shone green on trees. The sky was gray; the golden cupolas, shades of white. Strollers were raising a rumpus. Frieda Byelostok and Berta Vinograd were parading their fashions and grace.

On the bridge sat anglers. Greenish back yards were reflected in the dark water. Two beefy guys were bathing—and without hollering.

Savkina entered the little gates. It smelled of pine needles. Little copper icons hung on the crosses. One came upon inscriptions in verse. The yellow satin of Mari-Ivana's hat and the priest Valyukenas's flush were glimpsed fleetingly behind the bushes.

At home, they were drinking tea. A guest sat.

"Science has proven," Pavlushenka was boasting, "that there's no God."

"Let's allow," the guest retorted and, half closing her eyes, peered into his round face. "But how will you explain, for instance, such an expression as: 'God's world'?"

Smoothing out her skirts, Savkina took a seat. She poured the tea onto a saucer.

"I met them again."

"Not planning to switch to Catholicism?" the guest conjectured dreamily.

"Simpler," said Pavlushenka, waving his hand. The mother, smiling, threatened him with her finger. They had a laugh.

"Eat a little bun," the mother encouraged zealously. "American flour—imagine that you're in America!"

Savkina mourned over verses. Pavlushenka arrived from bathing preoccupied and, moving the tablecloth, sat down to write a newspaper dispatch about Babkina: "*Narobraz,* take note."

4

Savkina, tousled, lolled on the grass. Swatted mosquitoes. Plucked a little rose from a bush and smelled. She was tired—she had been detained to retype a report about the presentation of a banner.

Smiling pleasantly, the new lodger came out of the gate with shoes in her hand and headed for the cobbler's . . . Past the front garden walked Father Ivan.

"Rosa, Rosa." Into the house ran Pavlushenka. "Where's my newspaper with the article about Babkina?" Out of breath, he leaned out of the window. "Nyusha, where's the paper? He and I have made friends. How glad I am. He's divorced. Pays ten rubles for the child . . .'This stump,' he says, 'let's dig it out and chop it into fire-wood.'"

Bawling, an ice-cream vendor drove past. Kolya Yevreinov, in an embroidered skullcap, arrived. He fixed his shirt by the gate and cleared his throat.

"Go behind the sheds," said the mother in the room. "He's there with the new lodger's son: they've made friends."

Fedka, Garanka, Dunyashka, Agashka, and Klavushka were howling and tearing back and forth. The little doggy Kazbek was catching hold of their flaps. The mother in the house began scraping her slippers. The samovar chimney began to rattle.

"Go call to tea."

"He himself brought in," they were singing behind the sheds, "all the Communards for brutal, excruciating execution."

They were sitting embracing and slowly rocking. Savkina stopped: the third one was he, the puny one.

Yerygin

1

Yerygin, lying on his side, was bending and extending his leg. Its hair made traces in the sand.

A drum began to crackle. Pioneers holding five flags were returning from the forest. Yerygin was too lazy to go into the water again and instead rubbed the grains of sand off himself with his hands.

Little jacketless boys were running across the meadow and hurling a ball with their feet. "Phys-Culture," thought Yerygin, "the pledge of workers' health."

The bazaar was big. A stench hung in the air. Chinese were doing conjuring tricks. Metric tables were suspended on stalls. "Give, citizens, whatever you possibly can, if you have the possibility." Yerygin strolled up and down the rows to see whether any of the jobless were trading.

Before a lemonade stall crowded: Comrade Generalov, with a big, fat face, wearing a brand-new blue suit with four badges on his lapel; his wife, Fanya Yakovlevna; and his little daughter, Krasnaya Presnya. They were enjoying the weather and drinking lemonade. Yerygin bowed.

» «

Along a street overgrown with chamomile slowly shuffled the bishop, in a sailcloth robe and a little velvet cap, and Kukuikha, with a brocaded jacket on her arm.

"Cleopatra's a Russian name?" they were saying. "Yes." "And Victoria?"

Having dined, Yerygin rolled a cigarette of shag tobacco and settled down with the newspaper. Prominent German industrialist Mr. Wurst astounded by the state of our museums. "So much for your barbarians!"

Mother stopped in the doorway. "So how about going into accounting?" Her fustian dress reached the floor on the sides, but at the front, raised slightly by her belly, it was shorter. "Accountants are paid splendidly."

Yerygin put on a belt, took the buckets. Lyubov Ivanovna watched him from a window. Wearing a muslin blouse, she was groping the trench of hair twisted on her forehead with one hand, while gracefully twirling a peony with the other.

Facing the well, her tiny eyes squinting, white-breasted cashier Korovina, wearing a light blue housecoat, gazed. " 'Scuse me," she said. "You wouldn't know where the music's coming from?" "Returning from rapprochement with the Red Army," Yerygin answered and went off smiling. Geez, if only just to put down these buckets and whoosh right into her window!

In the evening Lyubov Ivanovna played the piano. After she'd played as much as she wanted to, she stood by the window, looked into the darkness, sighed, and from time to time touched her head to see whether the trench had come uncurled.

Vases gleamed on the chest of drawers: a pink horn of plenty in a gold hand, a light blue one in a silver. Mother was darning. Yerygin was recopying . . .

White bandits locked *nachdiv* Vinogradov in a shed. Nastya Golubtsova, wasting no time, ran off to get the Red Army. The bandits were executed. The *nachdiv* went away, and Nastya threw the icons out of her *izba* and enrolled in the RCP(b).

2

They stood holding flags before the train station. The sun warmed. The foreigners climbed out of the train and said speeches. Madmazelle Wuntsch, wearing a worn-out white felt hat tilted to one side, translated in a feeble little voice.

They had been traveling through various countries and nowhere had they seen such freedom. "Hurrah!" Music played, they celebrated, and, proud of their fatherland, looked at one another.

"Sovyet Répyoblick!"

"Réakshyon fashisht!"

Excited, they returned. Dispersed to their offices. Comrade Generalov sat down in his private office, with its sofa and Twelve Works of World Painting; Yerygin sat behind the grille.

Zakharov and Vakhrameyev came hopping up asking loads of questions. Corpulent, short-legged, wearing striped cotton jerseys. They'd, damn it all, overslept.

The jobless were admitted . . .

The sky had grown pale. Music began to thunder. Lyubov Ivanovna lit the lamp, curled the trench slightly, and pinned a mignonette to her jacket.

Yerygin took a little mirror off the chest of drawers, brought it up to the window, and took a look at himself: the white shirt with open collar suited him.

Maidens came out of gates and hastened off with their cavaliers, hurrying to the square for the flood benefit.

"Under the guidance of the Communist Party, we'll aid the workers of Red Leningrad!"

> Leningrad! A siren howled, it began to stink of smoke, pot-bellied industrialists descend from the steamship and walk to the museum. They are outstripped by sturdy sailors running to rallies. In a cabin window a lady in blue peeped out . . .

"Long live the leaders of the Leningrad proletariat!" Trumpets roared, flares flew off into the blackness, Bengal lights blazed.

Round-shouldered Korovina was illuminated, grinning, face whitened, with little pig eyes, and with her, cashier Yedryonkin.

Something sour wafted from the courtyards. Beyond the meadows, where the station was, lights clustered and dispersed. A wagon outstripped him without making a din, tires glittering.

Yerygin opened the gate. Over the shed floated the moon, half bright, half black, like a steamship window, its black curtain half-drawn.

"You?" Mother was astonished. "So soon!"

3

"Nastya" is going to be published. Keep writing . . .

The rider leapt down by Lyubov Ivanovna's porch. Flung himself toward the windows. She, radiant, came running out. The horse was tied to the picket fence. Yerygin grew pleasantly pensive. Recalled a line from a ballad. "Cinematograph," Mother laughed, and rolled up her sleeves to wash the plates.

The little gold sphere on the green cupola of the "October" Club glittered. Prickly grass seeds clung to the bottoms of trousers. A policeman with green collar tabs stood near the hairdresser's. A wax lady languidly looked him in the eyes.

Shaggy Zakharov and sleek, like a singed piglet, Vakhrameyev skipped onto the bridge, holding back their paunches with a hand underneath. Yerygin felt their muscles. They lit up shag tobacco. "We've enrolled in the accounting courses." "No," said Yerygin, "I've got something else in mind."

He left. They clambered onto the railing and plopped into the water.

Madmazelle Wuntsch, hunched up, was sitting beneath the willows. Hat tilted to one side, she resembled a brigand. Yerygin made her a salute. Madmazelle Wuntsch didn't see; she was dreaming, her half-blind eyes fixed upon the radiant west.

Trains passed beyond the meadows and poured forth sparks. It grew dark. Became damp. Yerygin was tormented: nothing from the life of the Red Army or executive workers would come to mind.

> The company advances, red, carrying little bundles and birch switches, it wants some *kvass* . . .
>
> A jobless person had created a scandal . . . forces his way in to Comrade Generalov. But he has Fanya Yakovlevna with Krasnaya Presnya on his couch—they've brought a cutlet. "Comrade, please leave this office! . . ."

But the extraneous, the unnecessary, kept revolving around.

Madmazelle Wuntsch, still young, is dictating in a feeble little voice: "The Germans are brutes." On the table is the oilcloth *Tercentenary:* the fat empresses, wearing medals, with bare shoulders and smiles . . . Good-bye. A horse roams. Bearded soldiers trudge in silence off to war. A lady stands by the roadside, slipping the soldiers jellies. She gives the last three pieces to Yerygin . . .

On the watchtower eleven was pealed. From out behind the rooftops came the moon—red, wan, crooked.

Yerygin was knocking at his door, gloomy. Lyubov Ivanovna, wearing a nightshirt, with little papers in her hair, leaned out of the window and looked: Whose door?

4

It would be stinking of cabbage in front of the "Narpit" cafeteria, and the panorama man, glancing every now and then over the top of his spectacles, would be strolling up and down around his box. Here Yerygin would slacken his pace and, turning his head, look in the window. Plates of bread and mustard pots could be seen. In the rear, the broad-shouldered cashier would be nodding off. "Have a look at the Belgian city of Liège?" the panorama man would creep up. Yerygin would rouse himself and run to accounting class. When he earns a lot, he'll come here to drink beer . . .

The clay grew mushy. Fanya Yakovlevna's galosh got swallowed up. The jobless weren't coming. Yerygin would bring stools together with Zakharov and Vakhrameyev and they would have a chat. Bringing their heads together, they would watch as Zakharov drew Germany under the heel of the Dawes Plan: rain, ducks floating, workers with shaved heads are lugging stones, overseers are cracking horsewhips, social traitors peep out from under an umbrella, rub their hands together and snigger.

Toward the holidays it froze slightly. Snow fell. On the seventh and eighth they had a good time. Mother too managed to get out to the "October" Club. Returning, she was spitting curses.

Storm clouds hung. They removed from offices the banners and garlands of colored paper: "Imperialist predators tormenting China! Get your filthy-bloody hands off a great oppressed nation!"

Beyond the river it was white—with little black shrubs. There was a ringing from behind. Peasants were driving cows toward him. Yerygin crossed the brook over the horse bones that had been thrown there in place of a bridge.

Hay carters trudged along. Slender stalks dangled and made traces in the snow . . . Something came back. Drum crackle, sand subtly traced with lines . . .

Along a green street with gray paths strolled the bishop and the Nepwoman, organizing a counterrevolution. *Intelligentka* Gadova is playing the piano. Comrade Leningradov, an executive worker, is falling in love. He rides to Gadova's on a black steed, listens to the trills, and drinks tea. Invites her to join the RCP(b), she—neither yes, nor no. What's going on? Now Gadova goes out to feed the hens. Comrade Leningradov is peeping into drawers and discovers the conspiracy. He steadfastly surmounts his love. The provincial health resort commission sends him to the Crimea. The court sentences the conspirators to capital punishment and petitions for its commutation to strict isolation: Soviet power does not take vengeance.

Konopatchikova

1

Casting tender glances, engineer Adolf Adolfovich was reading a report: "Ilyich and the Specialists."

Dobronravova from the Cultural Commission, hair closely cropped, with a shaved neck, was pacing up and down along the wall and reviewing a little pamphlet. The next speech would be hers: "Historical Materialism and the Liberation of Women."

Konopatchikova, squat, modestly looked right and left, inconspicuously got up, and slipped away. "Ache in the temples," she mumbled just in case, lifting her hand toward her graying hairdo, as though saluting.

Old women with birch switches trudged along, girded with towels. The ice-crusted snow crunched. It was growing dark. Lanterns burned without glittering.

A little bell was ringing. Women's Section rep Malkina, glancing from time to time at the passersby, was leaving on assignment.

The invalid Katz, sitting on a tall stool, majestically sold a bun. The switchman was blowing his horn. The entry onto the bridge was sinking into darkness, and, blazing up, a spark approached from there. The air suddenly was filled with the smell of shag tobacco, and cavaliers strode past with a song:

> A cold rain is falling, the wild winds freeze,
> Pushkin's leading some dame off into the trees.

» «

Locomotives hooted. Smoke rose slantwise and, illuminated from below, shone yellow. From out of the gates, exchanging remarks, came Vdovkin and Beryozynkina. They bowed to Kapitannikov's mortal remains and were important and solemn.

Konopatchikova had run into them here and there. She stopped and amiably said: "Hello."

They conversed in a low voice and smiled sadly: Konopatchikova, wearing a woolen beret with a little tassel; Vdovkin, broad-shouldered and nose-blowing; and Beryozynkina, meek, with a small head. The first stroke of the bell resounded. They fell silent and, pensive, lifted their eyes. Stars were shining overhead.

"Life passes by," Vdovkin sighed and recited a verse:

> Thus does the youth of life
> pass, leaving nary a trace.

The ladies were moved. He struck his lighter. A round nose was illuminated, and in the darkness the tip of a cigarette began to smolder.

They arranged to go to the filing works in the evening.

2

"Typist Kolotovkina," Konopatchikova, glancing at her watch now and then, was engaged in reading the provincial newspaper, "is passive and materially well-to-do.

> Why should she grind as a typist all day?
> She has a piano to happily play."

Galoshes began scraping in the vestibule. Vdovkin and Beryozynkina knocked.

They praised the room and examined the "Switzerland" lampshade and the playing cards with the gold edging. The aces had little pictures: "*L'egleez dez Envaleed,*" "*Statyu de Anree Katr.*"

"A little Parisian something," admired Vdovkin. "I myself like solitaires too," he was saying. "'The Queen,' for example, 'In Captivity,' 'The All-Seeing Eye' . . ."

"'The Country Road,'" prompted Konopatchikova.

Extending their arms before them, they went out. It smelled of incense. Courteous Vdovkin illuminated the steps with his lighter.

Upstairs doors slammed. Kapitannichikha ran out into the vestibule to keen over the deceased.

"And why'd you have all this stuff made," she lamented, "if you didn't want to wear it?" and stamped her feet.

> And why were you flooding the floor in the cellar with cement,
> if you didn't want to live?

They stopped and, having listened, slowly set off along the dark streets, looking around at the dogs.

"Life without labor," had been written over the stage in the filing works' theater, "is theft, and without art is barbarism." The orchestra played a quadrille.

The Swedish champion Jean Orlean, bellowing, tore iron chains and struck classical poses. Madmazelles Tamara, Cleopatra, Rufina, and Clara skipped and danced and, swinging their little skirts, cried out to the accompaniment of balalaikas:

> You'll need a union card
> in your possession
> if you want to enter
> a trade or profession.

'Eh," said Vdovkin, beaming as he swung his shoulders. nopatchikova was smiling and nodding her head . . .

It was freezing. A stripe of stars shone gray behind the filing orks' smokestack. An upright piano pattered. In the ventilation window steam twirled. Beyond the roses and ficuses, black against the bright background, they were dancing a zesty waltz, skipping and whirling.

"Happy," Beryozynkina crossed her hands upon her breast and grew pensive.

"They're," said Konopatchikova in a heartfelt voice, "reading a book, a very interesting one. The title's slipped my mind."

They had a talk about literature . . .

Smiling, full of pleasant thoughts, Konopatchikova gropingly found the edge of the lamp: the stars over the Swiss mountains and the colored lights in the windows of the huts and the little boat lamps blazed.

There was a scraping on the door. Wearing a big shawl, affected, Kapitannichikha slipped in. With modest grimaces, fingering the fringe of a shawl, she asked Konopatchikova to help tomorrow with preparations for the funeral repast.

"Don't say no," she was moving her flanks, fidgety, and pressing her head to her shoulder. "I'll flog his suits, and may everything turn out OK, properlike."

3

At Kapitannichikha's the ecclesiastical personages were coughing. The sacristan was fiddling with the censer in the vestibule. Konopatchikhova, passing through, took a little pinch of the smoke and sniffed.

» «

The cross on the bell tower glittered. The flag over the shopping arcades fluttered. Auntie Polushalchikha yelled and shook the Kapitannikov suits from time to time. "Is Maruska keening?" she asked, stooping and covering her mouth with her hand, and then, straightening back up, wearing a black coat made of little squares of plush, proud, looked around triumphantly.

Konopatchikova wandered about in anticipation. The sun warmed. It was squelchy underfoot.

Horses dozed. Soldiers in helmets, long-skirted and squat, jostled with the peasant women. "Middle" peasants, crowded together behind wagons, were drinking from a little green glass.

Engineer Adolf Adolfovich strolled alongside the houses in the sunshine, leading his little son in a striped cap by the hand. He screwed up his eyes against the light and smiled to the people on the porch, queuing, bent over, for his wife's dental office.

The funeral march became audible, and black banners came into view. People came running. Peasant men, whips lowered, watched. Peasant women, with little lace collars on their homespun coats and wearing Christmas tree beads, sighed.

There were lots of people. Kapitannichikha screamed from time to time. Vdovkin, joining in the singing, walked with Beryozynkina, her head inclined to one side. Konopatchikova followed them with her eyes.

"Sold," said Polushalchikha, pushing her way through, and she showed the money. They began making the purchases for the funeral repast.

They returned home on a wood sledge, their backs to the horse. The slush on the road glittered. Sparrows screamed. The bazaar disappeared into the distance. The confectioner Franz and the hairdresser Antoine, coming out to stand a bit in the sun, both wearing aprons, conversed . . .

Drops from the roof fell before the window. A dove-colored lilac smoke flew up over the locomotives. The fire made a noise in the stove. Downstairs, running his fingers over the strings of a balalaika, *rabkor* Petrov hummed somber romances. It was growing dark in the corners.

"Nikishka," Polushalchikha was saying and crying over horse-radish, "painted a 'Lenin' picture: it's a feast for the eyes."

On the coffee mill there was an oval relief with the Dutch queen Wilhelmina. Konopatchikova ground slowly, standing by the window. Growing pensive, she followed with her eyes the Chief of Police, showing off, galloping in the direction of the bridge and invalid Katz. Memories gathered.

4

Glasses gleamed and bottles, fat-bellied and slender, twinkled. Kapitannichikha, wearing a black dress, sleek, pious, stood by the table and, sorrowful, admired.

Konopatchikova, smiling modestly, curled and powdered, was sitting on the sofa and rolling into a tube a page from a calendar: an illustration of "Poverty in Germany" and two articles, "On the Benefit of Vitamins" and "The Theory of Relativity."

"Give thanks, Marusenka," instructed Polushalchikha and, spreading her hands, bowed deeply, as in *The Cornfield* in the illustration "Matchmakers' Dance."

The guests were entering. Konopatchikova drew herself up and watched the opening door in anticipation . . .

Spoons clattered and noses, broken into sweat over the soup, glittered. Polushalchikha, dressed as a cook, wearing an apron, was doing the serving. They bowed to Maruska, raising their little glasses. She would return their salutes, mournful, and drink up. There came a breath of acacia. Smiling amiably, the imposing Kuroedova arrived. "How are yours," she was being asked respectfully, "at the filing works?" "Are they," Konopatchikova began fussing, "still reading that book that was so interesting?" "*Tarzan*"? asked Kuroedova, swallowing . . .

Red, laughing blissfully, and dropping forks, they talked loudly. "It makes sense," Kuroedova was proving, "to buy lottery tickets. Ours, for example, recently won a toy cat, sherry, and a 'ham' money box."

Maruska was listening, pressing her hands between her knees and making her eyes round, like a quiet little girl, ingratiating, and she kept repeating, "Drink up."

Nikishka was shaking the hair that hung down onto his velvet jacket. "Art," he was exclaiming. Polushalchikha came from the kitchen and, taking pride, stood. "The mystery of colors!"

"Life without art is barbarism," quoted *rabkor* Petrov . . . A green scarf hung on his neck.

"I cannot," Vdovkin, growing pensive, began saying, "forget. In Kaluga we were staying with some Jews. They poured something into the samovar, and then an ineffable fragrance was diffused."

"In Vitebsk," said Konopatchikova, bent over, glancing into his face, "there's a coat of arms fastened to the train station: a knight on a steed. Nowhere, nowhere have I seen the like of it."

Beryozynkina, head thrown back, eyes closed, happy, was dipping the tip of her tongue into her glass and, moving her lips and smacking her chops, thoroughly enjoying herself.

Dorian Gray

1

Law Defender Ivanov—with paunch and little white mustaches—
stopped by and recounted two mysterious incidents from his life.

Sorokina, reclining against the chair back, listened absentmindedly. She watched indifferently and indulgently, like a lazy school-
teacher. Over the table hung a calendar and Engels in a red calico
frame.

People forced their way into shops. It stank of Lenten fare.
Rooks with twigs in their bills flew up. The hill on the other bank
was brown, but in winter it was a dirty white, lined all over with
slender trees, as though with streams of rain.

"Out before his company," soldiers were singing, "the commander nicely marched."

With a towel on her arm, Sorokina looked at herself in the mirror: under the eyes, wrinkles were starting to form.

Father arrived, merry, saying, "I've learned a recipe for making
shoe polish."

Mother placed the saltcellar on the table and swiftly approached the window.

"Pakhomova!" She was all curved over. She leaned back. Halted
and turned to look.

And, adjusting her black headdress, imposingly, like a lady in a
portrait in a provincial museum, she looked at Father.

He, dashing, with a pendent nose, like the tapir's in "Geography," stood before the mirror and wiped the stethoscope.

Storm clouds scattered. Old lady Gryzlova, wearing a black mantilla with laces and bugles, carried a church taper in a blue china candlestick. "Today's wind," she raised a finger, "'till Ascension."

Here and there a bell was struck.

Sorokina hesitated for a while. A beggar opened the door.

Slender candles illuminated chins. Ecclesiastical personages in black velvet clustered in the midst, before a lacquered cross.

"Pilate saith unto him! . . ."

Pakhomova, wearing a heavy yellow overcoat, not blinking, watched her candle.

Stars twinkled. The watchman, lifting up his beard, stood beneath the bell tower. "Nyurka, strike six times."

"I'd supposed you were an unbeliever," the snub-nosed registrar Millionshchikova came up.

A merry-go-round whirled, lanterns sparkling, and dangling its particolored pendants, slowly played a Cracovienne.

"A Russian, a German, and a Pole," crooned Millionshchikova.

The tavern shone. Reeling, clerks crawled out, "Vanya, don't fall . . ."

"Who's that?"

"Don't know. Spit-and-image copy of Dorian Gray—what do you think?"

Vanya. Cahors and Madeira, illumined by little lamps, were splashing within the bottles that were fixed in the revolving display. Vanya.

2

Nurses sat on the benches of the provincial stadium. A naked fellow in short little pants, gasping for breath, ran along the fence.

Sorokina stood up and, looking around, slowly set off.

"You wouldn't be Vasily Logginovich?" leaning against the gates, a drunk softly inquired.

A bosomy maiden thrust a note and started back. "Come hear the talk: 'What Christ died for.'"

Potatoes were flowering. Curtains stood out vividly on windows, bottles of cherries and granulated sugar had been arranged. Gramophones gurgled.

A corpulent old woman in a red jacket said hello: Osipikha the cleaning lady.

"Comrade Sorokina," she said, "I do apologize: what lovely weather."

The light blue and green expanses between the clouds paled.

On the peg were a strange cap and the Law Defender's monogrammed cane.

The samovar made a noise. On the tablecloth the reflected light from a bowl of jam shone red.

"Religion's the only thing that's left us," Mother was saying sincerely. "Pakhomova's affected, but she's religious, and so you forgive her."

And, holding a cup halfway to her lips, she peered at Father meaningfully.

He blew through his nose.

The Law Defender began recounting mysterious incidents. In a shadow on the writing table a skull showed its teeth.

Lanterns glittered beneath the trees. Musicians upon the stage would place their hands on their hips, have a smoke, and gawk. A waltz began to play. Stamping their feet, cavaliers danced decorously with cavaliers. Separating, they exchanged bows and shook hands.

Sorokina waited in the dark behind the benches.

There he is. Cap on the back of his head, slender . . .

If she were to stop him—"Vanya"—perhaps all would be explained: he'd muddled up, thought it wasn't at five, but at six.

"One doesn't get going at five, after all, when it's on for six."

She'd take him by the hand, and he'd lead her away.

"We'll go for a boat ride. I have a boat, the *Sun Yat-sen.*"

3

Mother went out to lock up. Wearing sandals, she stood squat, and her headdress could be seen from above, as on a saucer.

Old lady Gryzlova was taking a stroll, wearing a cape.

She stooped and scrutinized the leaves on the ground.

"Rough side up," she perceived, "good harvest."

Through an open window Sorokina caught sight of the back of her granddaughter's head. She was sitting at the piano and playing the waltz "Diana." Law Defender Ivanov, leaning against the window, was standing on the outside. Rocking his head, he was singing with feeling: *"de in jus vocando, de actionae danda."*

His conceited face was dreamy: Italy had crossed his mind, he recalled university.

Gossamer fluttered. Beneath the brown trees a church with dark blue corners shone white.

"Mama," a girl on the other side of the fence gossiped maliciously, "Manka's birching the piglet and scaring it."

The librarian looked at the people entering and divined: *"Jimmie Higgins?"*

Cavaliers in pressed trousers and girls in leather hats loitered along Leaders' Street. "In America advertisements are written on clouds . . ." They dreamed.

Osipikha, with a dahlia upon her breast, turned up in the public garden and tried to stir pity. "They say I'm a tramp," she grieved, "and I don't even know the roads."

"In the first ten-day period—a scorcher," a greenish little old man presented the newspaper, "in the second—incessant rains."

Millionshchikova took a seat alongside, saying, "Let's take a stroll in the field."

The light blue sky was fading. Slender little birds flew past over the earth.

"Remember," Millionshchikova glanced back and lowered her voice, "once in spring we paid attention . . ."

They were silent. In the city lanterns shone beneath the unextinguished sky.

They didn't part for some time.

"Those stars," Sorokina pointed, "are called the Septentriones . . ."

Father, lifting his eyebrows slightly, mulled over a game of patience. Mother was unstitching a raincoat. Sorokina opened a book from the library.

The clock ticked. Struck. Ticked.

A dog outside the window was barking winter style.

"Dorian, Dorian," had been printed here, there, and everywhere in the book.

"Dorian, Dorian."

The Nurse

Leaves lay beneath the trees.

The moon was dwindling.

Little crowds carrying flags descended toward the main street. Ice sparkled in the meadows beyond the river, and little black figures darted about on skates.

"Hullo," said Mukhin, as he touched his cap. Smiling, he ran down. Above his knees he ached from soccer.

There was jostling before the Palace of Labor. Comrade Perch, cultural officer, stood on the balcony with her secretary, Volodka Grakov.

"Woldemar—my non-indifference," Katya Bashmakova was saying and looking Mukhin in the eyes . . .

Finally setting forth. Music playing. Gilding glittering on red calico. Sky over the white office buildings a dark blue.

Forming up on Victims' Square. Buried here were Kapustin's grandmother and, separately, Comrade Gusev.

Covered with canvas, something scraggy stuck up.

"What if that's a skeleton there," sniggered Comrade Perch.

The piece of canvas was pulled off. Flags lowered. The orchestra began to play. There was fidgeting by the monument, people were boosted onto the rostrum.

"Comrade Gusev brought to a near-resolution the tasks confronting the Party."

They turned this way and that. Behind was the cemetery, to the right—reformatory, in front—barracks.

53

Chubby-cheeked, wearing a scarf, the nurse, sticking her tongue out, licked her fingers and squinted.

Mukhin took a close look, broke ranks, and lay in wait.

He was being admired: slender, trousers turned up, green socks above his shoes.

Dispersing began. Gusev's father, wearing an overcoat like a little barrel, with a belt and fur collar, buttonholed Mukhin.

"What a work!" he reached out his hand to the obelisk with Comrade Gusev's head on its point.

The nurse was leaving.

"I've got to," rushed Mukhin. "Pardon."

The way was barred. Trumpeting, marching, burying Syomkina the suicide, expelled for instability. "You fell a victim."

Her girlfriend, candidate member Grushkina, howling, watched from her gate.

"Disciplined," praised embezzler Mishka-Dobrokhim, "not taking part in the procession."

The nurse disappeared . . .

Smoke ran beyond the meadows and divided a strip of forest into two: near and distant.

Cramming hands into pockets, Mishka, replete, whistled softly.

"Let you out?" Mukhin started and congratulated him.

They descended. Greeted those met. Stopped by the placards.

"I'm going home," Mishka excused himself. "To have dinner."

A rainbow sparkled on the edge of a mirror in the window of the "Tezhe." A "Moscow Miss" was arranged all around—soap, powder, and eau-de-cologne: she steals her way into someone, muffles herself in ermine, the night a dark blue, snowflakes . . .

One longed for the extraordinary—to go away somewhere, be a cinematograph actor or a pilot.

In the cafeteria Mukhin sat for a long time over the newspaper. The memorial unveiled is a model of monumental art . . .

The sun was setting. Churches turned pink.

Steps pounded across the frozen clay.

It grew dark in the room. A schedule shone white over the table: phys-ed, politico-ed . . .

In the landlady's living room Katya Bashmakova sang languidly and strummed a guitar.

Mishka arrived. Listened. Made a sly face.

"No," Mukhin dolefully shook his head, "I never like anyone who likes me. And there's never any of whatever I like."

"That's right," agreed Mishka.

Stars shone. Someone was whispering by the gate. Leaves rustled underfoot.

Walking arm in arm. Pensive, singing:

> Let's clean, let's clean,
> let's clean, let's clean,
> let's clean, citizen.

They went down to the river: it was still, the white streak from a star.

Looked in at the bathhouse and regretted not having brought sunflower seeds, or else they could have sat here awhile.

A bit of jostling by the cinematograph: a count converses with a lady. Hurried to get a ticket . . .

In the "Mosselprom" cafeteria music rang out. A little lamp burned mysteriously. "What do you eat at a desert picnic?" they were saying at one table. "All the sand-which-is there."

Behind the counter dozed the Ukrainian girl, wearing a brown tie. They encouraged her, "Cheer up!"

So as not to pick anything up, they rinsed their glasses with beer. Clinked.

"I almost got to meet the nurse," said Mukhin.

The Medass

The man got off the train, extracted a small mirror, and took a look around. The telegraphist who had been waiting by the bell came running up to him.

"Medical attendant?" she asked and stood, like a child, looking at him. He raised his eyebrows, which joined on the bridge of his nose, and looked indulgently.

"Medass," he bowed.

It was slippery walking. He took her arm.

"Ah," she marveled.

The little fountain by the station was full, and spray flew with the wind beyond the cement pool.

"This way." Sheds showed up darkly from three sides, and a ripple ran across the puddles. Grass could be seen through the ice. They ran up the stairs, took off their coats in the kitchen, and hung them on the door.

It was dark in the little room. The mother was breathing behind a screen.

"Wake her?" the telegraphist tiptoed out after peeping there.

"No," he gallantly waved his hands a few times. "It's a long time until the train, let her sleep." Turning, she stole away to the kitchen and began to rattle the samovar. Cyclamen was blooming in a pot. The medass sniffed. Beneath the window ran a road, and straw lay scattered about. Beyond the wattle fence there was snow, and sticking up out of the snow were beet leaves.

They drank tea and talked quietly about the city.

"An interesting life," the medass delighted, "Mary Pickford acts splendidly."

He looked at the fire and, smiling slightly, was pensive. His eyebrows were raised. A little hair, uncaptured by the razor, shone beneath his lip.

They moved to the sofa and sat in the shadow. The stove warmed. The samovar would fall silent and again begin to cheep.

"Jenny Jugo's a brunette," the medass burst forth and listened, spellbound himself. "She's the portrait of you."

Drawing in her legs and huddling up, the telegraphist kept silent. Her eyes were half-shut and dark from pupils that were dilated, as under atropine.

"You've a chill," the medass looked closely. "You've caught a cold. Spring has done you ill." "No, I'm fine," she said, as her teeth began to chatter, "perhaps the ventilation pane."

He turned to look and shook his head. "Closed. Put on your coat. I'll give you a sudorific. Must look after yourself, dress properly, before going outdoors—eat." She stood up and began to wash the dishes, tapping against the slop basin. The medass got up, walked up and down on tiptoe, took some music off a table, looked at the name, and began humming the romance. The mother awoke.

The Father

On the pilot's grave was a cross: a propeller. Interesting paper garlands lay here and there. The pot-bellied church with its windowpanes knocked out watched from behind maple trees. A round bench skirted a linden.

The father was walking with his boys through the cemetery to the river. Beyond the bushes, where the hops were, the mother was buried. "We'll visit her afterward," said the father, "or else we'll be late for the waves."

A horn began hooting. "Faster," the boys shouted. "Faster," the father began to hurry. Everyone broke into a run. Over the gate stood an angel, painted on tin plate and engraved. In their hurry they forgot to stand for a while and, heads lifted, admire it.

As they ran down the path, the horn once again rang out. "We'll be late," the father urged. Hearts hammered, and there was a banging in their heads.

Shedding jackets, they arrived at a run and, pulling legs from trousers, fell to the ground: made it. To the right came a rumbling, and smoke was approaching; the steamboat's prow, white, came into view from behind the bushes. They leapt up, started to dance, began waving their caps. The majestic captain was giving orders.

The paddle wheel was making a racket, its foam sizzled, its wake seethed in the water. They squatted, because women were watching from the deck, and, peering at them sideways, they squeezed their hands with their knees.

"Smack," the first wave hit the shore. "Quickly!" Everyone flung themselves in.

The river was like a sea. "Ooh," people were yelling and jumping up. "Ooh," the father was yelling, holding the boys in his arms and leaping. "Ooh, ooh," they were yelling, clasping him by the neck and squealing.

The waves ended. The father, hooting like a steamboat, was moving through the water on hands and knees. The little kids were riding him. Then he washed, and they took turns scrubbing his back, like grown-ups. Straightening up, he looked himself over and moved his muscles: in the evening he was supposed to go see Lyubov Ivanovna. He was thinking, "But on the other hand, I'm not a bad father."

They walked back slowly. "Or else the bathing," the father was saying, "will have been for naught." They clambered up the path for a long time. Blew on dandelions and plucked chamomile petals. Turned and looked downward. Cows were walking along the shore, shining in the river. Sometimes they would moo. Little lamps lit up by the station and their light played. The sun set. The stars were not yet visible. The angel over the gate had grown dark.

"You wait here a bit," said the father by the linden tree. "I'll be back." They took a seat, removing their little caps, and linked arms. A mosquito whined.

The bushes were blending together, black. The tops of crosses thrust out from them. The hops showed. Here the father came to a halt and stood without his cap. He had stopped by in regard to

Lyubov Ivanovna and was vacillating: How and what to say? But the little boys were scared. The dead were lying beneath the earth. Someone might peep out from the church's broken windows, a hand might reach out. It was nice when the father came.

Walking the streets, soft with dust, was pleasant. Lanterns burned here and there. The little stalls gleamed. In courtyards women conversed with their decorous cows, returned from the herd. In the municipal garden firemen executed a waltz. The father bought a cigar and two gingerbreads. Silently, they enjoyed themselves.

The Sailor

Lyoshka jumped out of bed. Mother was on duty.

Bending, as over a well, the half-circle moon barely shone white. A straggly birch with dark branches did not stir. Droplets sparkled on the grass. Pecking here, there, hens with chicks roamed the yard.

Belly swinging, wearing a black housecoat with blue roses, Trifonikha descended the stairs. In her hand was a key, and on her arm hung a handbag embroidered with a tiger.

"Ugh," Trifonikha looked sideways, "little pig!" and, self-important, set off to get buns.

"I washed," Lyoshka shouted after her.

A water carter with a big mustache, taking a bite from a pound of sifted-flour bread, made a rattling noise with his wheels. Dust rose drowsily and settled once again.

"Uncle dear," Lyoshka asked sweetly, "give me a ride." The water carter let him sit up on the barrel. Envious were the women carrying bunches of clay jugs of baked milk on yokes, the conductress wearing glasses who was driving a cow and raising a rope over it threateningly, and the four petty thieves sitting beneath a hillock and sorting through bags of linen.

"Robbed an attic," the water carter pointed and helped Lyoshka to the ground.

The sun had risen and was scorching hot. The sifted-flour bread in Silebina's teashop was illuminated. The kid from the cinematograph was pasting posters. "Free Admission" was printed on them, but Lyoshka didn't know how to read.

Sitting on a bench beneath the cherry trees in a little garden with a brown fence, a sailor basked in the sun and played a balalaika: "Transvaal, Transvaal . . ."

It was nice by the garden. The fence had already heated up and was warm; one's shoulders were warmed from behind, it smelled of clover.

A sailor . . .

But Mother had already returned and was combing her hair before a shiver of mirror.

They drank boiling water with granulated sugar and bread. They puffed. Mother commanded not to go down to the river and, drawing the curtain, lay down to sleep.

Suddenly music rang out. Everybody rushed.

The tips of banners sparkled. Drums crackled.

Pioneers wearing ties were marching to the forest. A *kvass* wagon rumbled behind.

After them! along with the boys, along with the doggies, waving arms, skipping, hopping:

"To the forest!"

Alongside the gardens, twirling a loofah, came the sailor. His light blue collar fluttered and two narrow ribbons flew about at the back of his head.

A sailor! The music, moving away, died down, and the dust settled. Lyoshka's heart pounded. He ran to the river—after the sailor.

A sailor! They came running from all over. Those swimming crawled out. Lollers on the sand leapt up.

A sailor!

Brown, like a clay jug, he sprang, came to the surface, and swam off. On his arm was a dark blue anchor, and his muscles inflated—like the twisted sifted-flour bread on Silebina's shelf.

"I'm the one who brought him," boasted Lyoshka.

It was hot. The air over the river streamed. Fish plashed. Boats drifted past, women in colored bands stooped over the side, lowering fingers into the water.

Bathers wrestled, turned somersaults, and walked on their hands.

But the sun was advancing. Formerly behind, it had gotten in front; time for dinner.

Mother was waiting. The potatoes had been boiled, the bread and the oil bottle were on the table.

They stuffed themselves. Mother praised the oil now and again. They lapped their spoons clean. Went out onto the stoop.

In the yard, blankets spread about, sat their neighbors. Rocking little children, humming softly, searching with kitchen knives in each other's hair.

"We'll get ourselves set up too," said Mother, as she grew happy and ran to fetch a blanket.

They lay. Lyoshka put his head on her knees. She went through his shaggy hair with her fingers. Little cloudlets in sailors' jackets flew past across the sky, cloudlets resembling sifted-flour bread and heaps of linen.

One felt like sleeping, and yet didn't feel like . . .

"Mommies," Mother leapt up, "if we're gonna bathe, let's get bathing: we'll be late for the free admission."

Free admission!

They jumped up one after another, began scurrying, tied up their hair, and ran out the gates. Racing one another and laughing, and then growing quiet and singing wistfully:

> The poor man's clothes cling to the roots,
> boughs plaited themselves in his hair.

They plucked the tough tall grass in order to place it under their feet when they came out onto the bank. A bitter white juice leaked out and began to dry on their fingers.

Threshing with their legs, they swam and, yelping, squatted. Lyoshka, standing by the water, squished through the mud. The sun was setting. Mosquitoes started to bite. Frogs began to croak. The sky faded. The grass grew cold. Dust in the ruts lay warm and heated one's feet. The street seethed. Everyone was hurrying to the free admission.

The water carter came along, casting glances from on high, as from atop a barrel, and twirling his mustaches.

Swinging her hand, as if there were a rope in it, the old conductress was hurrying, and the four petty thieves who'd robbed the attic ran merrily.

There was a rumpus. Lines stood for the ice-cream vendors. A sunflower husk crackled. In the garden, lanterns glittered, music played, and a fountain gushed. Mother got lost. Kids weren't admitted into the cinematograph. Lyoshka began to howl.

It grew dark. The music circled low, beaten down by the dew. Silebina sat on her stoop—still, still, pensively, not raising the towel threateningly, not yelling. In the garden, in the dark, the sailor softly strummed his balalaika: "Transvaal, Transvaal . . ."

He, just like Lyoshka, wasn't at the free admission—darling . . .

Sighing, Trifonikha strolled about the yard and, admiring a little star, chewed. From the bag with the tiger she drew out a pie and held it out to Lyoshka.

Sitting on a step, he began eating, cramming it into his mouth with both hands. The pie was sweet, but his hands were salty from the mud and bitter from the grass he'd plucked while going to the riverbank with Mother.

»»» «««

Palmistry

Petrov breathed the heavily perfumed air with pleasure and, counting those waiting, sat down. Ladislas excused himself and moved away from the man he was shaving and shot the bolt. "I made it," Petrov laughed, thinking this a good sign.

The barbers shaved in silence—tired, they were hurrying and not uttering courtesies. Scissors tinkled. Christmas was coming. The bells had been taken down and no longer droned outside the windows. "Peeh," a truck sometimes cheeped in a bass and ran past, shaking the street.

Petrov wasn't reading. He was skimming. He'd already studied this book with the palms depicted on every page. He'd finished it yesterday evening and, shutting it, had sat down before a looking glass and recollected the verses he'd once learned in school:

> Discharged be the duty that God bequeathed
> Unto me, a sinner.

Trimmed and clipped, he left. He smelled fragrant. His mustache, small beard, and the ringlets of fur at the corners of his collar got covered with rime. A lofty moon sailed in a green circle. The hard-packed snow overflowed with brilliancies. As in the daytime, the placards on the walls were distinct. Petrov had already read them: the model museum "Science," with its departments of gynecology, mineralogy, and Sacco and Vanzetti, had reduced its prices.

Margarita Titovna lived nearby. Petrov laughed. As usual, she'll sneak off to another room, her mother will call her, she'll come, yawning and swaying, and make a sour face. Unembarrassed, he'll take hold of her hand, turn it palm upward, read what was and what will be, whom to avoid. She will listen spellbound . . . "Margarita Titovna," Petrov sang in his mind, exulting and swaying his torso slightly.

Conversing loudly, two friends wearing Finnish caps ran past arm in arm. "I made her an insulting proposition," heard Petrov, "she didn't consent." He fell to thinking: she didn't consent—an omen, possibly inauspicious.

And it was true: Margarita Titovna proved not to be at home. "Done gone to the museum," the mother sympathized. "Vespers going ain't the fashion now," she laughed. "Yes," sighed Petrov. "A mouse got the better of me," the mother said, entertaining him with conversation. "I've fixed lard on a hook in the trap: sure to be caught now." "He'll be caught," Petrov guffawed.

Steps squealed. Wires and branches were white.

Churches with dim little windows watched the moon.

The museum shone. Delightful pictures, red from the red lanterns, hung by the entrance. The Bulgarian woman had died, lying on the snow, and the regiment of soldiers adopts her daughter. A gorilla, drawing the vines apart, steals up to the bathing maiden: *A Woman's Abduction*. Petrov stepped behind the curtain and wiped his glasses clean. "A ticket," he demanded, twisting his mustache and touching his beard, the palmistry peeking from his pocket.

»»» «««

As You Wish

The veterinarian had taken two rubles. The medicine had cost seventy kopecks. It had been of no use. "Go see the crone," the women advised, "she'll help." Seleznyova locked the gate and, wearing a kerchief, tucking her hands into her cuffs, stooped over, squat, in a long skirt and felt boots, set out.

There was a presentiment of thaw. The trees were black. Garden fences divided the hillocks' slopes into crooked quadrangles.

Factory smokestacks emitted smoke. There stood new houses with rounded corners. Engineers with little pointed beards, wearing caps with badges, self-important, sauntered about. Seleznyova stepped aside and, stopping, looked at them: she was paid forty rubles a month, while they, it was told, got six hundred.

Burdocks stuck up from under the snow. Gray fences sagged. "Auntie, heh," little boys yelled and slid past her feet on sleds.

The yards down below, with pathways and apple trees, and the meadows and woods in the distance could be seen. Smoldering pieces of wood lay by the crone's gates. Seleznyova rang. The crone, with the dark ringlets on her forehead fastened to her kerchief, and wearing an overcoat, opened to her.

"Look at that little pine," said the crone, "and don't think." The pine shone blue, thrusting itself up over a patch of forest. The crone muttered. Music played at the skating rink. "Here's some salt," the crone nudged Seleznyova, "you add it to her . . ."

The nanny goat bent down over her drink and turned away from it. Hanging her head, Seleznyova went out. "That's where you are," said the caller, squat, wearing a homemade hat. Seleznyova greeted her. "He's coming to take a look at you," the caller announced. "I would advise it. The deceased was a swanky one, everything at his place is intact—a house full of things." Lifting the lantern from the ground, they set off, embracing, slowly.

The visitor arrived, wearing a sealskin cap and a brown overcoat with a lambskin collar. "I do apologize," he was saying and, eyes shining, smirked into his graying mustache. "On the contrary," Seleznyova replied. The caller was enjoying herself, gazing.

"Time flies," the visitor marveled. "Spring's not far off. We're already learning May's hymn.

"Sisters," looking at Seleznyova, he unexpectedly began to sing, waving a spoon. The caller nudged Seleznyova, beaming.

> Put on the wedding dress,
> strew your path with garlands of roses.

"Brothers." Swaying, the caller joined in and winked at Seleznyova so she'd not lag behind.

> Open wide your arms to one another:
> the years of suffering and tears are past.

"Splendid," the caller exulted. "Marvelous, true words. And you sing superbly." "Yes," nodded Seleznyova. She didn't like the visitor. To her the song seemed stupid. "Good-bye," they said, finally bidding farewell.

Throwing on a *katsaveika,* Seleznyova ran out. It smelled of damp. Music drifted from afar. The nanny goat didn't start bleating when the lock began to rattle. She was lying on the straw, not stirring.

It was dawning. There was dripping from the rooftops. It wasn't necessary to bring anything to drink. Having washed, Seleznyova left so as to get everything arranged before going to the office. A man from the market hired on for fifty kopecks and, seating herself in the wood sledge, Seleznyova rolled up with him. "'Course she's alive," he said, entering the shed. Seleznyova shook her head. Little boys ran after the sledge. "Dead goat," they were yelling and skipping. People dispersed. Stooped over, Seleznyova dragged up the sleigh with the box and began raking out the flooring.

"Hello," yesterday's visitor suddenly turned up from behind. He was smirking, wearing the sealskin cap made from the deceased's muff, and his eyes shone. His cheeks were glossy. "Your gates are wide open," he was saying, "I was off to school rather early, why not, I'm thinking." Setting down the rake, Seleznyova pointed to the empty enclosure. He sighed courteously. "I cry and I sob," he began crooning, "scarcely see I death." Eyes downcast, Seleznyova lightly touched the shed wall with her fingers and looked at them. Drops fell on her sleeves. A crow cawed. "Well, then, right you are," the visitor stuck out his mustache. "Won't detain you. I, you see, want to send a woman to meet with you—to have a talk." "As you wish," said Seleznyova.

The Garden

Delegates to the district congress of the Union of Medical Labor Workers were sitting on a bench and talking about politics. Little travel baskets stood between them. The morning sun warmed. Sprawling, they were stretching their legs in a state of bliss.

Smiling, the women delegates were slowly walking around the flowerbeds. They were looking at the flowers, inclining their heads to one side. "And next year it will be even more lovely," the gardener Chow-Din-Chi was saying. The delegates, touched, encircled him. "Can you turn on the fountain?" they were asking.

Chernyakova chuckled, gazing at them. "Just look at that," she said. Wearing a red necktie, ringlets of hair above her wrinkles, she sat beneath an acacia. "Mister Chinaman, here's what I'll tell you," she beckoned. "Today, we're going to be burying Taisiya, the cleaning woman: you will please come." "With enormous pleasure," answered Chow-Din-Chi, and Chernyakova rose and shook his hand. "We're counting on you," she bid farewell and, picking a blade of grass, turned and left, purring.

Poetess Lipetz ran into her, and she stopped and greeted her amiably. "My compliments, Comrade Lipetzkovaya, where are you hurrying?"

Dusting off the bench, poetess Lipetz sat down and settled back. Her verses had been printed in today's paper:

"with sirens is met the day. Working folk . . ."

She, to the accompaniment of the fountain's plash, declaimed them.

Troubles awaited Chernyakova. She had been notified that she would be fired if she received visitors. She began to wail. "It was the coachman who informed," said she.

The coffin holding Taisiya arrived from the hospital. The coachman secured the horse by the reins and went to announce it. The office supervisor had given the clerks leave to see off Taisiya. They formed up behind the coffin. Chernyakova, straightening her tie, took her place with the trade union rep, behind them stood the registrar with the courier, and behind them, the typists, Zakushnyak and Poluyektova. "Gee up," shouted the coachman and, holding the ends of the reins, set off beside the cart. The wheels began to rattle across the cobblestones. The trade union rep waved his arm and six voices began singing. Chow-Din-Chi crossed the garden with a handbell and showed the visitors out. He locked the gate and caught up with the procession. Chernyakova glanced back at him. Pensioner Zachs, tapping with her stick, came running up to him and asked who the deceased was. "The District Council of Professional Unions' cleaning lady," answered Chow-Din-Chi amiably. "I know her," said pensioner Zachs joyfully. "I worked together with her when I was Secretary of the Union of Education Workers." She walked mincingly in order to fall in step and began singing, raising her head like a hen swallowing water. The sun scorched. Dust crowded into their mouths.

They buried Taisiya. Leaping up onto the hearse, the coachman rolled off. The girls set off running: the Secretary of the Union of Medical Labor Workers had given them each a delegate's voucher for dinner in the cafeteria—one had to grab places before the seasonal workers assembled. Pensioner Zachs, hopping along, walked with the Chinaman. Chernyakova was returning with the trade union rep.

"Comrade trade union rep," she was saying courteously, "I'm being informed on, but just think what rate I get: twenty seven rubles."

There was no longer anyone in the District Council of Professional Workers. Only the Executive Secretary of the District Intersectional Bureau of Engineers and Technicians, Comrade Lipetz, electrical engineer, still sat. He had put in an application for a raise and had begun each day to be detained. He was holding a newspaper. There was his portrait, his little article, and his daughter's poem:

"with sirens is met the day. Working folk . . ."

Chernyakova locked all the doors and looked at him. "Comrade Lipetzkov," she said deferentially, passing her hand over her lips. "I'm leaving now, or else the seasonal workers will come a-flying. Hang the key in the telephone room, if you would be so gracious. I have a key collectionator, a key tillery there."

It was hot. The sidewalk had softened. Carts, bringing bricks to building sites, rumbled. The registrar, the courier, and the typists Zakushnyak and Poluyektova had already eaten and were trudging along, all a-steam, picking their teeth with their tongues. They exchanged winks with Chernyakova. "Good?" she inquired and began to hurry. Educated people were eating decorously, spreading their fingers and chasing off flies. "Novozybkov" was engraved on the palm tree tubs. Looking glasses were hanging on the walls. Across from Chernyakova an attractive cavalier was paying compliments to a maiden. "You're lemonades yourself," he was saying, pouring her out a glass, "only rosy red." "Am I really so rosy red?" she marveled. "Ugh, look at that," Chernyakova chuckled and, finished eating, wiped her lips off with her tie and left, repeating that conversation.

Trying to outstrip one another, bearded, the seasonal workers flew in her direction. She opened the windows in the District Council of Professional Unions. Air burst in. Meadows could be seen beyond the rooftops, herds made a splash of color, naked boys ran along the river. Chernyakova tucked up her skirt, rolled up her sleeves, and began cleaning up. "You're so rosy red," she was saying, making a nice smile and chuckling.

The carts stopped rumbling. The horse artillery division, the police reserve, and the sewage disposal men galloped past by turns toward the river; dust rose and darkened the sun. Dim, it descended toward the monument's cloth cap. The garden was full. Women were standing by the fountain and wandering around the flowerbeds. Men, sprawled, were sitting in their "*toile-du-nord*" shirts. Volleyballers were hopping, returning the ball with their heads. Pensioner Zachs was following after the Chinaman.

"I can imagine how bored you must be with us," she was saying. Chernyakova came up and listened with sympathy. "Taisiya has died," she said, coughing.

The clouds turned crimson and faded. The Union of Medical Labor Workers congress closed and began to sing "Arise." Flowers began to scent. A loudspeaker started shouting hello. It grew dark, became difficult to keep an eye on the visitors. Chow-Din-Chi walked up and down with the handbell. He locked the gate and set off to see Prokopchik. Pensioner Zachs and Chernyakova accompanied him. Lanterns rocked gently. The smell of hay flew in from the meadows. In the optician's window stood plaster cast heads wearing glasses, and in their glasses electricity would now blaze up, now go out. "Mister Chinaman, that is beauty," said Chernyakova.

"Wonderful things," agreed Chow-Din-Chi. Pensioner Zachs, frowning, took her leave. "Don't think I'm tired," she cautioned.

Raftmen's campfires burned by the river. The moon was rising. The gold letters of the District Council of Professional Unions water station glittered. Late bathers splashed in the dark. Prokopchik was sucking a pipe. He was glad of the guests. "My compliments," they affably greeted. "How are you getting on?" they asked and shook his hand. "A Department of Culture official flew in," he recounted, "demanded that everyone wear short pants." They shook their heads and laughed. In the city lights were burning. The water murmured. "The coachman is informing on me, the son of a bitch," complained Chernyakova. "Eh," she said, and the words began to play on her lips, and she started spinning, howling with laughter. The men stomped in accompaniment. The tie flew about.

"You're so rosy red," she brought forth and shook her sides, stamping, and yelped.

Poetess Lipetz, face turned toward the moon, was strolling, and her father, the Executive Secretary of the District Intersectional Bureau of Engineers and Technicians, was strolling with her. They were strolling after watching a performance, delegate tickets to which they had received from the Secretary of the Union of Medical Labor Workers. Poetess Lipetz's scarf fluttered. Gazing upward, she rocked her head and softly declaimed:

"with sirens is met the day. Working folk . . ."

The Portrait

1

As always, coming from the well, I found the landlord in the yard.

He was shaking a samovar over a washbasin and, as always, he jested amiably, nodding at my buckets, "Fyzz-ed."

As always, taking leave of Maman, we went out and, in the entryway, flinging open the gate, Father, gallant, made way for me. By my shadow I saw that I was hunched over, and so I straightened up.

Churches stood. Streets descended and climbed. Old men sat on their earthen mounds. Droplets sparkled and, plopping down onto shoulders, splattered. As always, at the turn, touching his cap, Father took his leave.

The four four-story apartment houses came into view, the square with lanterns and loudspeakers. Greatcoats tucked up, soldiers with rifles were running, throwing themselves onto the earth and leaping back up. Standing on the porch and exchanging glances, the office girls looked them over. Hats were reflected in the polished columns.

Praising the weather, we settled down. Abacuses began to click. Comrade Shatskina, wearing a "Solferino" jacket, walked past and inspected us. The sun was shifting. The shadow of an airplane ran across the tables, and we had a talk about how much pilots earn.

After dinner, washing finished, Maman changed and, wearing gloves, decorous, departed.

"We're electing a deacon," she stopped and looked imposingly at Father and me.

"Splendid," we praised.

Father, squinting, rustled the newspaper. Branches crisscrossed outside the window. In the stable, on the other side of the fence, a horse shifted from side to side.

Guests knocked and, unfastening the muskrat around their necks, squat, joyously looked up at us from down below. A flower brooch and a dagger brooch glittered. "I'll go tell Maman," I said, escaping.

She, solemn, as in a photographer's studio, was sitting in the school. Old ladies whispered. A candidate for the deacon's post, wearing riding breeches, was orating.

"I am of proletarian origin!" he exclaimed.

Motley charts with Gothic letters were on display: roadway, two thousand square meters; lanterns, twelve; watchtower, one.

"But did you study in a seminary?" Maman asked, standing up. I called her.

The little pools in the tracks were skinning over. People came leaping outdoors without coats and caps, they were closing shutters. Little boys were talking, sitting on a porch, and their skates dangled and tinkled.

Moscow's Street—formerly Moscow Street—was stirring. Buses bellowed. Cabbies turned back their carriage rugs. Mounting the church porch, I bought a ticket. Palm trees stood. Little fish opened their mouths wide. Cavaliers were stamping, lifting their chins, and sticking out their little bows. I hung around among them.

Richard Tolmedge was shown wearing a sleeveless jacket and little short trousers. He was undergoing treatment for love, and a doctor examined him.

"Darling Richard," we smiled and glanced at one another, beaming.

On top of the program, the musical satirists "Fiss-Diss" played the trumpet on birch switches. "Donkey, donkey," they would cry, "where are you?" and then answer, "I'm in the Presidium of the Second International."

Colliding with passersby, I chased after him. "Listen," I wanted to shout. He walked, swaying, rather short, with a raised collar and wearing a cloth cap with a flap.

Father stopped me. He too had fled the guests. "Is Richard nice?" he asked, and by his voice I could see how he had slightly raised his eyebrows. "And the ideology acceptable?"

A narrow moon shone behind the branches. Little gaps on the shadows brightened. Wild dogs slept on the snow.

"Yes, yes," I nodded, and wasn't listening . . . That one, in the cloth cap, in the crush at the door, he had groped me.

Maman, eyes half-shut, with a towel on her shoulder, washing up the cups, was smiling. The guests had just left: it still smelled of boot grease.

"Well," Maman said to us condescendingly, "you don't know anything. The Poles have taken Polotsk. A letter has come from Ukraine. She's decided not to give us any meat."

As always, we sat down. The cat, rocking the chair, was licking herself beneath her tail. Father rustled the pages. Maman, chuckling softly, sewed lace onto pants. I was looking through a book. Anna Chillyag, all hairs, was pacing and carried before her a flower. Paul Kruger was smiling. This the guests had brought.

2

On the porch, mysterious, the landlord detained us. "Came to blows," he said. "Lunacharsky coshed Rykov."

We came out. Little puddles loomed darkly by the gate. Stretching their necks, hens were drinking. Cavaliers came running past and whistled softly from time to time. Their haircuts were showing, coming out from under their hats. Droplets sparkled on their shoulders. A boy was smearing walls, sticking on posters and smoothing: Metropolitan Vvedensky is coming.

DOES GOD EXIST?

Father took his leave. An airplane droned. A flag fluttered, fastened at the corners, and the sky between it and the pole shone blue.

Electricity had been conducted to the sign over the theater. The electrician, hand up to his eyes, was walking across the roof and swaying, rather short. "It's he," I thought. "What's up there?" people asked me, stopping. I got jostled. There was the smell of nail polish. Flanks arched, coquettish Ivanova, wearing a red hat, greeted me. I made a pleasant face, and we set off. "Spring . . . ," we had a chat.

At twelve, while, looking in the little mirror that had been placed on the table, she was having a bite to eat, I approached her. A salami was lying on newspaper. "And beat up," I perused, "a female citizen who had been passing along Moscow's Street." I coughed modestly.

"Will you be at the soirée?" I asked.

Everybody was dressed up. Fragrances wafted. Little papers had been fastened to the lamps. Conifer needles rained down. A sponsored "middle" peasant sat with Comrade Shatskina and coughed.

Phys–edists performed in violet sleeveless blouses, lifted their arms; the hair in their armpits would show. A choir sang.

Balalaika players, raising their eyes, began strumming. We swayed slightly in our places, dancing with our torsos.

Comrade Shatskina, contented, looked us over. "All right," we blinked and clapped our hands. The friendship unit stamped along in accompaniment.

It's quiet,

As when I was little, a waltz began to twirl,

all around,
and the wind sobs on the knolls.

"I'll be going to the lecture," said Ivanova, ceasing to watch the door, "to see if anything's going on there." She extracted her powder: a lake with water lilies and a swan.

It was freezing cold. Two big stars, like buttons on the back of a coat, sparkled. Over the theater, red, coloring the snow on the square and the air, letters glittered. People in cloth caps were walking past.

I looked at them closely.

A garden bloomed on stage. A nymph behind a shrub shone white, covering its breast. Metropolitan Vvedensky was retorting to Petrov, an atheist of province-wide importance. We examined the spectators. Father sat, yawning. He nodded to me. "The guests," he explained.

"There he is," Ivanova began beaming and nudged me. Zhorzhik from the electric station had spotted us.

"Electrician," he introduced himself to me.

"Let's get out," said Ivanova. In the foyer, standing reflected in the marble walls, she reproached him beneath a palm tree. He was trying to vindicate himself, lifting his eyebrows. "I wanted to come, what's the matter?" he was saying. "But, just imagine, the laundress got me in trouble." "Oh, you're hopeless," Ivanova said, languidly turning away.

Squabbling, we descended to Moscow's Street. It reeked of gasoline: it recalled the Nevsky, with automobile beams and snowflakes circling in them.

From the grocer's, treading on others' footprints, we paced as far as the pharmacy and turned. A policewoman stood modestly, in a belt worn high. A horse shook itself, and a little bell winced.

"Pushkin, where art thou?" someone was saying up ahead. Embarrassed, Ivanova burst out laughing. "Comrades," said Zhorzhik impressively, "it's embarrassing." "Get lost," they said, turning to look at him.

Removing his cap, he bowed to all sides. "How do you do?" he exclaimed. I watched closely.

Near the big apartment houses, Father caught up to me. He was saying something, laughing, and shrugging his shoulders. I assented and chuckled, not listening attentively. It was empty in the lanes. The stars and hearts carved into shutters shone.

"In Knopp's store," they were singing around the corner.

Maman was animated. There was the smell of boot grease and pomade. A Bible lay on the table.

"Everything, everything is prophesied here," Maman told us joyously, as she watched meaningfully.

3

Maman listened closely. "They're coming," she said, leaping up and brushing her breast with the tips of her fingers, as one shakes off crumbs.

As always, we went out to wait beneath the pear trees until it was over. The Easter cake was visible. A cineraria stood on the windowsill.

"Christ," began tinkling in the house. A church smell came flying. There was ringing all around. A cat, gazing upward, tracked airplanes. There began a trampling on the steps. The clergy, donning hats and swinging its waists, descended, and Maman, majestic, nodded to it from the porch.

The landlords came and wished us a happy holiday. "You are welcome," Maman made them sit down. Everyone was smiling. "I'm off to visit my patients," said Father. I too slipped away. Forks and knives chattered in my wake.

Families were strolling. Little children slept in their arms. Bells were ringing.

"Holidays," said placards that had been pasted all over, "are days of Esenin-itis."

The guests were mincing, stooped over, hastening to visit us, wearing sumptuous jackets and turbans made of shawls. I turned into a little garden, ungracious.

Leaves rustled—last year's. Blades of grass were pushing through.

"In Penza," there was a conversation on a bench, "all the women are immoral."

Ivanova stole up, poked me with a finger, and said, "Kkh." She smelled fragrant. Calico violets adorned her.

"I drew good fortune," she laughed.

The gate banged. Soviet workers in rubber coats were entering. Popping open the handbag, we looked at ourselves in the little mirror. The clock struck. "I know," Ivanova got up, "where he is."

The loudspeakers on the square wheezed. Cavaliers in brand-new suits, hands on one another's shoulders, clustered over a hawker's tray. They were tapping eggs together. In a window gleamed a banner with a quotation, and a rope, covered with little red papers, hung. We entered. It reeked of greasy books. Propping herself up, the librarian was sitting behind the counter. A lady in profile stood out vividly on her collar.

"Your cheek is soiled," said Ivanova. "It's from gunpowder," she answered and watched proudly. The Society of Friends of the Library was meeting: Zhorzhik and the glass-engraver Prokhorova. Wearing sky blue, she was chewing something oily, and her face shone.

Zhorzhik was distracted. Inspired, he ruffled his hair. "Damnation to you," he was painting a sign, "Mister Trotsky." There was the smell of the hair oil "Violettes de Parme."

"Political slagons?" approaching, Ivanova asked gloomily. I stood aside. *Virineya* and *Natalia Tarpova* lay on the recommended table. In the newspaper I found Comrade Shatskina: she was walking in the ranks. "Away with Pessimism and Unbelief," said a little placard she was carrying; "Poincaré, take that in the kisser," a flag fluttered over her.

Rain poured. The door opened. Everyone looked. "Grishka from the gardens," Prokhorova announced.

Rather short, he stood, shaking off a cloth cap with a flap . . .

From the main room, seated on a chair, the attendant watched us. We clinked glasses, feeling shy. Paper flowers had been arranged on the tables.

"To yours," Zhorzhik gallantly hoisted and knocked it back. "A pity," he grieved, taking a bite, "that singing's not permitted here: how wondrous that would be." "Yes," we agreed, and the attendant sighed in the other room and said, "Proheebited."

"You're an alien element," Prokhorova said, "but I like you." "I'm glad," I thanked her. The lamps dimmed little by little. Voices blended. Candor and friendship were what was desired. Ivanova arose and shook Prokhorova's hand. "I'm coming," I said, and then ran off.

Stuck to the window, the landlords eavesdropped. The cineraria cast a shadow upon them. Behind the curtain spoons tinkled,

Maman was arguing imposingly, and the guests, moved, were telling her yes.

I was going off, stumbling. "Crocked," they said, turning to look at me. Tittering, sovcomworkers were saying in a whisper, "Kabuki." Loudspeakers softly played.

In the theater, as always, there was shooting. The bootblack was packing up his case. Ice-cream vendors, dispersing, rumbled.

There was a din on Moscow's Street. Cavaliers clustered on the church porch, buying sunflower seeds.

In the foyer the palm trees shone black. The little fish opened their mouths wide. The orchestra thundered. The spectators leaned against their ladies. Ali-Vali cut off his own head. He set it on a plate and, bracelets jingling, carried it between the rows, smiling.

"Not a miracle, but science," he elucidated. "There are no miracles."

We exchanged glances in amazement. There was shoving at the door. Hissing, a rocket flew up. The stars over the pharmacy shivered.

I remained alone. There was ringing in the darkness. Laces clacked against shoes.

A Ukrainian troupe was stamping, crying out, "Hup." The provincial militia reserve was undressing, sitting on beds.

Sleepy dogs lifted their heads. Some lights were reflected in the flood.

In the gardens it was still. Nothing could be seen. The dampness was penetrating.

4

Pears fell, thudding. The landlords would spring out and, falling on them, snatch them up. On a ladder placed against the fence they would climb over to the neighboring yard and return with apples: *jus tollendi*.

The mailmaid opened the door and shouted. I took the newspaper. Tsilia Lazarevna Rom was changing her name. The bourgeois picture *The General* was getting torn to shreds: Why doesn't Buster Keaton portray a northerner?

"Happy holiday," Maman arrived. She looked demonstratively and, sighing, thrust her prayers for the dead behind the mustard pot.

The trees were yellow. Leaves stuck to heels.

"Rakhilya," the bootblack crooned melancholically. Muscles were bursting his jersey open. Hair shone black in the slit of his collar. Shoelaces, hung by one end, swung. "You're destined for me."

In the Culture Garden the flowerbeds had lost their bloom. "Wishing Citizens to Buy Flowers," the notice boards had not been removed, "Possible from Gardener." The little "goose" fountain plashed from time to time.

Wrestlers sat, arms akimbo. Wearing fashionable hats, they recalled foreigners from gripping dramas. Female citizens, burning up, would rise and shake their fleshiness from time to time.

At the circus a whip cracked. Horses flashed beyond the open door. A horsewoman would come hopping.

Prokhorova came out of the buffet with the world champion Slutzker. They were finishing chewing something, and her face shone.

Ivanova wasn't there. A social activist, she was working on the committee for Comrade Shatskina's farewell party.

The military sciences circle was studying behind the acacias. "The most," the lecturer knit his brows, "lethal gas—I've forgotten its name—begins with a fuh." Pencils squeaked.

Zhorzhik hid his notepad. Wearing a "Jungsturm" shirt, he adjusted himself and approached me, courteous. "Warm day," we spoke a little and were silent awhile. Prokhorova, perfidious, was visible to him. "But it's already been freezing," said I. "Indeed," he answered, "the temperature has been exceeding . . ."

"Autumn. . . ," we said our good-byes.

There was crowding on Moscow's Street: the aviator's funeral was anticipated. A green sphere glimmered in the pharmacy. On the windowsill stood a perfume bottle with the Neva and the Fortress.

A bus began to honk. Through the glass the passengers watched us with absent eyes. They were going on.

Carts with potatoes arrived. "Our Answer to the Chinese Generals," a poster explained. Comrade Shatskina stopped, smiling, and her cook, wearing a blue *kika*, loaded down with baskets, stopped behind her.

The landlord, one arm set out to the side, was carrying kerosene in a can. "Off to the Jordan?" he asked, grinning, as always, and fawned a bit. The wild beasts in the circus tent were crying out. A musician with a bunch of flowers on his chest was making ringing sounds on vodka bottles. "Bridge Dangerous," a sign cautioned. Anglers, silent, twirled the little handles of their fishing rods with a reeling motion. Laundresses with red legs were bending over the water. Willows shed their leaves.

Gossamer had clung to hummocks in the meadow. Geese ambled. Skulls and bones had been painted on electric poles.

I sat down near a big stone, about which I knew from the newspaper that it was desirable to use when putting up a monument. Narrow leaves floated. New apartment houses, shining white on the hill, were glittering glass. Cabbage heads in gardens rounded, like green roses.

Phys-edists moored, undressed and, well brought-up, turned somersaults in their undies. Then they discarded them and ran, chasing one another and playing leapfrog.

I got up, growing pale. It was he—not the electrician, not Grishka, but that very one, with the flap.

"Listen," I wanted to shout.

"Photograph?" he asked smartly, turned around, bent over, and touched his knee joint. "There's a portrait for you," he said, showing the palm of his hand.

I moved away majestically. A lion snarled. Playing shrilly, the funeral was moving, invisible, beyond the river.

Material

Godulevich received a challenge to a competition and mulled it over. Two points she accepted, two she declined, and to one she introduced an adjustment.

According to the competition, she was supposed to conduct work among the masses out-of-doors. Closing the library, every evening she would move to the garden with several books and spread them out attractively on a little table at the end of a path. With the deposit of a document one could take them and read under a lantern.

She would sit. The movie projector would crackle. The orchestra would play from time to time. Boys would sometimes come running up and make erotic signs at her with their fingers or watch her through the cardboard eyeglasses, resembling masks, with red and green lenses, that had been given away at "The Miracles of Shades." Once two cavaliers walked past the table, conversing about cream soda.

When it struck ten, Godulevich would leave. Cracoviennes and mazurkas would resound in her wake. Sometimes the moon would be shining, and sometimes storm clouds would hang and lightning would blink in the distance. From the windows of the venereal hospital, lit up from the room, people in unbuttoned shirts would thrust themselves out. "Give us a smoke," they would beg. God-ulevich would run away in fear. Shoes pounded. "Still working," her landlady would say to her, unlocking, and she'd go to bed.

On days off she'd go to the picture, if it was a drama. When a comedy was playing, she'd sit in the yard on the ice cellar. She would read, and down below people would walk about and roosters would cry. Guests would come to visit engineer Sidorov—engi-neer Smirnov from the communal section and the old lady Paskudniyak from the *tsey-eyr-ka*. Malinnikov would appear at the window with his violin, frowning, and play "Kol Nidrei."

Evening would come. Sometimes carts would rumble. Music would come flying from gardens. A door would open. The Sidorovs, standing on the threshold, both lanky, would wave after their guests. Appearing white in the darkness, they would wave back.

One day Smirnov returned. "Say," he said, "have you heard the new couplets, 'Lenin loves kids'?" He looked around and began singing under his breath. Drawing nearer, Godulevich coughed. It grew quiet, the door shut, and the guests dispersed.

The days were long and the weeks short. There came and went campaigns concerning cooperation and an antimilitary one. "Working outdoors," wrote Godulevich in her application for a place in a vacation home, "I didn't slacken work in the winter premises either. As a result my nerves have become somewhat upset." And, indeed, she had become irritable and almost swore at library subscriber Reks, who had requested a songbook.

》 《

In the newspaper there appeared an announcement concerning a purge in the communal section. Godulevich sat down and took up a pen. She had decided to come forward there with the material concerning Smirnov. So as not to forget anything, she composed a note.

Wearing a blue dress with little yellow stripes, she set out. The venereals watched her from the windows. Portraits of the coryphaeus Stepanyants and the prima ballerina Pravednikova had been pasted on the corners. She came upon subscribers who touched the peaks of their caps.

It was crowded at the purge. The chairman was a jokester, and the spectators were rolling in laughter. The communalists were sitting gray in the face. Smirnov was holding a newspaper before him. Turned green, he was blowing on his hands, shoving them under himself, standing up, and going out. Godulevich pitied him. "The hell with him," she thought.

She had repented of this faintheartedness when she arrived from the vacation home, grown heavier by eight pounds, dark and noisy. But it was no longer possible to rectify anything. In her absence engineer Smirnov had left together with the Sidorovs for Tajikistan, whence engineer Khozyainov had informed them by telegraph of small towns with deficit goods and a salary of a thousand seven hundred.

The official instruction concerning winter cultural work had already been sent, and the club director had promised to give it to Godulevich to read. Old lady Paskudniyak, smiling timidly, would come at sunset and sit in the courtyard. "When they were loading," she'd laugh, beaming, "remember? People came running and watched." "I was away," Godulevich would say and tell her about the vacation home. Old lady Paskudniyak would listen spellbound, still. Malinnikov, wearing suspenders, would approach.

She would tell how much butter they would give there and what a pleasant conversationalist Comrade Shatsky from Klintsy had been. She would tell how she'd come up with a note for the live newspaper and how she'd gone to look at the village with Elga Nokhimovna Rog: the crops had been harvested, and it was spacious all about; a lizard had run out from under her feet; covered with straw, *izbas* had come into view—sleighs and sledge runners had been lying about beside them.

Tea

They were delivering speeches: both parent Pekhterev, town soviet member ("I'll speak to you very briefly," he had warned), and the director, glancing upward from time to time, like a coloratura soprano performing a number after a movie drama, as well as the instructors, called aunts, and Red Army man Misha from the friendship unit, blushing, and Pioneer Kolya, speaking in a deep voice, and Gavrik from the children's playground. They were trying to persuade Agafyushka, the collective farm worker, to give a talk. She would not assent.

"Kiddies," the doctor then rose and coughed. "We are transferring you to the school. But there's no cause to be anxious. There will be a doctor there as well, and he will be providing you med-aid."

Cook Daryushka got up, straightened the kerchief on her head, and remained silent for a while. "Kiddies," she said dolefully, "are you pleased with me?" "Pleased," they answered. "Have I offended you?" she continued to ask. "Abused you? Dishonored you?" "No," they cheeped in chorus, moved to pity, "no!" Everyone was touched.

The ceremonial part had concluded. The presidium came down from the stage.

"Misha," the children began to shout, surrounding the Red Army man and hanging on him. Pioneer Kolya frowned and, moving off to the side, was jealous. Parents clustered by the walls, scrutinizing the children's works hung there and the "construction materials" in a chest in the corner. "Aunt," they'd sometimes beckon and ask for explanations.

"Kiddies," the director called, appearing in the cafeteria's opening doors. On a table behind her a samovar and mugs could be seen. "And for the parents," she smiled blissfully, "tea will be later, when they take away the children."

Everyone looked at one another. For the parents! What a surprise. "But I, perhaps, won't be able to come the second time," announced Gavrik's mother. "What shall we do?" the director asked of her in hesitation, beamed, and, taking her by the waist, seated her to drink with the children.

Happy, after drinking their fill, they sang. "We'll come back," the parents were saying, going away. "Farewell, children," exclaimed the aunts.

Pioneer Kolya and Red Army man Misha were each given a candy and, while the tidying up was going on, were asked to wait in the orchard.

The sunset was red and the antennas over the houses recalled the "stakes for sticking skulls on" in travel books. The white reformatory appeared a dark blue. The imprisoned, leaning against the bars, were singing lengthily, "Ah!"

Red Army man Misha picked up an apple and presented it to Kolya. "How's it going, brother?" taking him by the shoulders, he asked, and Kolya fell in love with him. They got into a conversation. Time flew unnoticed. Radio reports rang out from open windows. Dispersing from the stadium, passions inflamed, footballers, invisible behind a fence, were squabbling.

The tea was a gala event. They drank decorously. "The pirogi," the aunts explained, beaming, "we baked ourselves, but the *zhamochki* were allotted at the *tsey-eyr-ka.*" It was nice. Shaikina and Porokhonnikova enumerated the items issued from the restricted-access store. Everybody livened up. It grew noisy. Daryushka, leaning on her elbows, was questioning Misha about what Red Army men have for dinner. Agafyushka grew merry and was telling about how she goes out to work while she herself is afraid, lest the homestead be burned.

Parent Davidyuk had brought his accordion with him. It lay there, metal plates gleaming. They moved into the big room, and Davidyuk took a seat and crossed his legs. A waltz began. Straightening his tie, Kolya ran off toward Misha to ask him. But Misha, clasping technician Nastenka, was already twirling around and whispering something to her. Daryushka was laughing and nodding at them. The aunts, letting their little heads drop to one side, danced modestly, taking one another by the hands.

"Let's look for apples," whispered Shaikina to Porokhonnikova. Dancing, they slipped out. On the porch was Kolya. Not looking around, he stood facing the darkness. The doctor was sitting, huddled up. Nudging each other, Porokhonnikova and Shaikina stopped. A star broke loose and streamed, as though it had leapt down by parachute. It was quiet in front and there was the tramping of feet behind.

Pekhterev, town soviet member, appeared on the porch. He scratched his head. "A whole assembly," he said. "But for some air," explained Shaikina, giggling. They had a talk about water boxes: the town soviet had resolved to break them up and install vending machines with a little hole for half-kopeck pieces. A pince-nez flashed. The doctor grew agitated on the bench. "In America," she began to fuss, "vending machines are everywhere: you drop a coin, and chocolate leaps out." "You don't say," they answered her.

No one parted. Everyone wanted to outwait the others. The doctor spun out the thread, telling about America. There, when speaking on the telephone, you can see your interlocutor. There the sidewalks move, there the steps of staircases ascend together with the people walking on them. She talked and talked, to the strains of the accordion and the tramping, and didn't know how to stop talking, even though she sensed that no one believed her.

Old Ladies in a Small Town

1

Tow-headed twelve-year-old Hieretiida, wearing a blue dress and black apron, hopping, carried a spade on her shoulder. Behind her, bony arms folded on protruding belly, majestically walked Katerina Alexandrovna, wearing a broad black dress with white stripes and a little black hat with a crepe tail. Behind, carrying a particolored feather broom, a box holding a fan and an umbrella, strutted Dashenka, forty years old, dark, bosomy, and conceited.

On the balcony, red from the heat, fat-fleshed, wearing a sky blue housecoat with laces, sat Pferdchen's missus, drinking coffee with *pfefferkuchen*. Her legs were obstructed by a sign:

VON PFERDCHEN'S APOTHECARY

ART. TSYPEROVICH

Katerina Alexandrovna moved her lips and started looking into the distance; Dashenka, craning her neck, gawked: Pferdchen's missus is a profligate.

They turned to the right and on the little bridge with the sign "Bridge Dangerous" came out onto a green street with gray paths.

Hieretiida was staring at a girl who was running into the wind, holding a pillowslip stretched on a frame over her head. Katerina Alexandrovna was looking fixedly at the Countess's park, with its cobblestone fence.

The frail excise official, wearing a long, yellow calico-print shirt, was digging in the front garden. The excise official's gaunt missus, wearing a blue overall, barefoot, was filling a watering can. Katerina Alexandrovna narrowed her eyes. "They and their frivolous ideas."

Boys were bathing beneath the railway embankment. Rafts slowly floated. A black cow, standing with its front legs in the water, fanned itself with its tail.

Gavrilova was sitting on the porch. Seeing that somebody was coming, she got up and went into the house: she'd recently thrown herself into the well and now was ashamed.

Katerina Alexandrovna called to Hieretiida in a rasping voice, and they turned to the right and set off for the cemetery along a path between the vegetable gardens.

Around the grave they kindled two little fires to protect against mosquitoes. Dashenka cleaned the bench with the broom. Katerina Alexandrovna took a seat, sat awhile, looked at the monument with its portrait of an old man wearing medals and epaulettes. They put out the fires.

They returned along a different road. Beyond the field began the Countess's cobblestone wall. Passing the gates, Katerina Alexandrovna turned her head and looked at the courtyard with the round flowerbed and the white facade with closed windows; she caught sight of no one.

By the gate of the public garden she released Dashenka and Hieretiida and, eyes half-shut, drawing in the sweet air, entered beneath the flowering lindens. Paths led to a little square with four benches. On one side, in a striped stall, white with red, gnawing nuts, sat Rosa Klyatskina. Around her were arranged bottles of *kvass*. Tsyperovich, wearing a brown velvet jacket, arms crossed on chest, stood on the outside and, striking poses, looked into Rosa's eyes.

Frau Anna Rabe, wearing a muslin dress with little blue bouquets, smiling pleasantly, came out onto the little square from a different alley. Before her ran the pug Zodelchen. Katerina Alexandrovna, fanning herself and holding back the crepe, settled down with Frau Anna in a manner so as not to see Rosa and Tsyperovich. Zodelchen, now and then nibbling the grass, ambled about.

The sun had set behind the lindens. The dark verdure seemed transparent. The wind, dying down, stirred little hairs that had escaped the coiffure. Balyul, with his rather pimply face, slipped past, stooped over. "Probably from the palazzo," said Frau Anna. Katerina Alexandrovna blinked. "Yes, after all the Countess, it seems, has come . . . Tell me, dear Anna Frantsevna, are you and she acquainted?"

"When my Karlchen was alive, he was treating them at the palazzo, then I also with them was acquainted. But when they showed to me their fanatismus, then I no more with them am acquainted."

She began to tell how Karlchen had been dying, and Count Bonaventura had been trying to persuade him to embrace katholizismus. "There was entire schkandal, and the Countense Anna and I are not now very agreeable." Katerina Alexandrovna hastily got up and said good-bye.

2

A warm, wet wind was blowing, the road had turned black. Katerina Alexandrovna was coming from Mass. "This wind," she was saying, "is blowing from the sea. Smell—there's a whiff of salt and sailcloth. I like how it's said in Acts: 'A tempestuous wind, called Euroclydon.'"

In front of the Roman Catholic church was the sleigh from the palazzo. "Dashenka, Hieretiida, go ahead. I'm going back . . . forgot . . ."

The crepe, sewn onto her hat, was flying up and stretching out, striking her in the face. Her nose had become red, tears streamed. Beggars crept up and, wailing, held out their hands. A tall old lady, wearing a red fur coat, with a rosary on her neck, snub-nosed, came out of the church. Katerina Alexandrovna licked her lips and made a dash. "Countess! Is it you that I . . . what chance!" "Pleeze makes way," the Countess intoned nasally.

Snow crunched beneath soles. The sun warmed the nose and left cheek. Little white puffs of smoke were rising up over the roofs. The morning moon waned. "Look, Dashenka and Hieretiida," Katerina Alexandrovna pointed, "it's bowed, as though over shattered dreams." "Sure enough," answered Dashenka.

The canary was chirping, the little doggie Elza was warming herself on a pillow by the hot stove, on the floor lay quadrangles of sunlight together with the shadows of ficus leaves and the light shadows of lace curtains. "Ardently beloved Anna Ivanovna," said Katerina Alexandrovna, "I wish you a happy angel's day."

They took a seat on the divan beneath the wall carpet with the Spanish woman and Spanish men. The name day celebrant, beaming, was stroking the satin ribbon on her housecoat with her short fingers. "The excise official's missus—have you heard?—went back. She'd been hiding at Gavrilova's. How do you like that? I've invited Gavrilova to dinner: she'll be telling about it." "Oh, these frivolous ideas . . ."

"The Countess has been riding about: yesterday she drove past twice, today she drove past."

"Just as though she were in a subjugated town," said Katerina Alexandrovna.

The guests, faces red, were at a loss what to say. "I was already lying down to sleep," Gavrilova was saying, "suddenly a knock. She appears. 'Let me live here awhile. My sister will send some money, and I'll leave for Kaluga.' While we were talking, a puddle melted around her big feet. Then—worse. Now she starts pestering me with the *Reading Circle:* 'When were you born?' And my birthday's the first of April. And so that's what I answer. 'So let's,' she says, 'read the *Reading Circle* for April the first.' 'Oh, go to hell!' Fortunately, she didn't have much money, and from her sister, of course, zilch, no answer whatsoever, and so back she went."

Katerina Alexandrovna, solemn, wearing black silk, moved the raisins aside, stood up, wiped her mouth, and in a voice full of emotion said, "Poor you, my Praskovia Alexandrovna. How much you've suffered from that good-for-nothing . . . My ardently beloved, I've grown fond of you. Accept my friendship. After all aren't you my sister: I too am an Alexandrovna." Her lips quavered. She thought, "And I'm just as lonely as you."

Anna Ivanovna clasped Gavrilova in her arms and loudly kissed her. Frau Anna Rabe stood up and, smiling pleasantly, presented Gavrilova with a little bouquet of mignonette. The priest's missus and the district police officer's missus clinked glasses with Gavrilova and shouted "hurrah." She, perspiring, laid her hand on her heart and bowed.

"With joy I see," Katerina Alexandrovna began squeaking, "how unanimously we are disposed now. I should like us to remain in such unanimity forever . . . Before our very eyes people ride about precisely as though in a subjugated town. Let us unite and repulse." The guests were listening, heads hanging, and through the coffee steam peered at her with dulled eyes. "What then, Anna Ivanovna," asked the postmaster's missus, "shall we arrange the little green table or are we going to disperse?" "Yes, it is time, I see," said Katerina Alexandrovna, and, majestic, she pinned up her shawl under her chin. "Praskovia Alexandrovna, let's go. You'll sit awhile at my place, we'll have a little chat . . ."

It was growing dark. There was the smell of smoke. At the end of the street, where a dark blue storm cloud had torn away, a yellow stripe brightened in the sky. Katerina Alexandrovna kept silent. Gavrilova was animated, rocking back and forth.

3

In Frau Rabe's front garden daisies broke into blossom. From Petersburg came Marya Karlovna with family: three little girls with braids and a nanny. Katerina Alexandrovna met them at the gate. "Ah, Marie," she said, "how glad I am. Go, lie down, and then we'll talk at length." She took a seat at the table and began to write on a scrap of paper what to ask and what to tell. After tea she invited Marya Karlovna to take a stroll and, coming out past the gate, glanced at her note. "Well, Marie . . ."

"Auntie dear," said Marya Karlovna, "we'll unite them yet."

Blue and green intervals brightened between clouds. From the gardens it smelled of jasmine. Bathers were returning with faces grown pale and wet hair. Over the Pferdchens' roof a little white star could be seen.

The next evening, after washing the tea service, Marya Karlovna examined her fidgety figure and, running her palms across her jacket and white linen skirt, threw a scarf over her head. "I'm going."

They began to go boating—with food and guitars, walking to the woods in a crowd. Returning, they'd drop by the public garden, where four musicians with long noses would be playing on the stage. They'd request the anthem. Everyone would rise and remove their hats. For a minute it would become silent. Lanterns would crackle in the silence. Rosa Klyatskina, gnawing nuts, would rise in her stall. The solemn music would sound, people would shout "hurrah" and "encore."

Katerina Alexandrovna participated little in these divertissements. She was contemplating her will. Every day after dinner she would clamber up the hill, overgrown with stiff grass with yellow flowers, and stroll before the decorated chapel: Herod was having a bite to eat with guests . . . The sliced-through neck of Saint John was red on the inside with little white circles, like the sausage on a Tsyperovich sign. Katerina Alexandrovna would roam between the campfires and watch the road: Would not a little procession appear, would not the Countess Anna come walking with the priest Balyul and the two old ladies in red capes? Leaving the old ladies down below, where Dashenka and Hieretiida hum softly and search in each other's head, the Countess would clamber up, leaning on the priest, and give him a sign to stop, and approach and bow her head. Katerina Alexandrovna would say, "Hello, Countess."

They were kissing the cross. The ecclesiastical personage was holding the cross and exclaiming, "Glory to Thee, God, glory to Thee, God." Dashenka and Hieretiida were locking the pillow for genuflection and the rug in the cupboard next to the candle box. Katerina Alexandrovna, waiting for them by the entrance, was eating the host. She was approached by a greenish little old man in a brown coat: Gorokhov, Chairman of the Municipal Brotherhood of Saint Alexander Nevsky, familiar by hearsay with her activities . . .

They sat in the public garden. Katerina Alexandrovna, without a hat, wearing a broad white dress with black stripes, was fanning herself and smiling. Gorokhov, lisping slightly, was telling about the Brotherhood, how it walks in the procession, had sent a telegram to Tsarskoe Selo, organized a concert, and gilded the big cathedral chandelier. Katerina Alexandrovna, playing with her fan every now and again, was looking at the trees. "Absolutely, absolutely," Gorokhov was trying to persuade. "You could order a banner, and it would be kept in your living room, and in processions it would flutter over your heads, just think, what splendor, no?" "Let's take a stroll," invited Katerina Alexandrovna.

They walked along the river. There was the smell of clover. "A chapel," rejoiced Gorokhov. "John the Baptist! There's just the name for you: the Brotherhood of Saint John." Katerina Alexandrovna said, "The view from here's not bad."

They were returning. The palish blue sky grew lilac and pink. They turned and looked at the two red ovals: above the river and in the river. Their yellow faces and gray heads were lit up by the red light. "Katerina Alexandrovna," Gorokhov was exclaiming pompously. "This spectacle of the two suns, does it not speak of two brotherhoods? Of Saint Alexander and Saint John! It's splendid." But Katerina Alexandrovna was thinking not of two brotherhoods, but of two ladies: majestic, wearing light-colored dresses, pinkish from the evening's rays, they watch from the hill and, moved, utter refined phrases . . .

In town they were unveiling a monument. The ladies, dressed up, set off. Gorokhov met them at the station. "No Katerina Alexandrovna? What a pity! Monsignor wanted to have a word with her concerning the Brotherhood. They would have their own banner—ah, how splendid . . ."

He placed them by the railing, behind which, under the canvas, stood something scraggy. "I'm afraid," said the district police officer's missus coquettishly. "What if that's a skeleton there?"

Soldiers had been arranged all around. A little gold sphere on a green cupola glittered blindingly, and, if one squinted, scattered needlelike rays all about. A peal of bells began. Stooped, banners clambered out and straightened back up. The icons, the clergy's costumes, and the epaulettes beamed. The bishop in sky blue velvet garb with silver galloons approached the railing. The canvas was pulled off. On a little cement block stood a cannon, with its barrel pointing upward, and on it an eagle wearing a crown. "Lovely, lovely," the ladies chirped, swerving from the sprays of holy water, and spread their elbows out wide, so that the wind freshened their sweated flanks.

During refreshments in the tent it was very lively. It was guaranteed that war would begin tomorrow or the day after. It was pondered where to flee. "It's okay for you, Frau Anna: you'll tell them that you were born in some Berlin or other, and that's the end of it." "Need one lie?" asked Frau Anna. "I've never lied." "Good gracious, and where will I go," Gavrilova was thinking.

"I'll go with you to Petersburg," said Katerina Alexandrovna, after listening to the report from Marya Karlovna. "I was about to even so. It has become loathsome here—nobody to talk to."

The table was being set for supper and forks clattered. Katerina Alexandrovna was standing on the veranda. "To Petersburg! . . . You're ambling along the companies and see the blue cupola with the stars. Dragging themselves along toward the Warsaw Station are hay carters with baskets at their feet. It stinks of burning from the grub houses. Old women trudge to night service, wearing cloaks, wearing mantillas embroidered with bugles . . ."

The moon stood over the fence, half bright, half black, like a steamship window, half-covered by a black curtain. "Anna, Anna, you didn't want me to draw back the curtain that shut you off from me . . ."

War had not begun. Marya Karlovna's husband arrived. He would walk to the river to sunbathe. Returning, he would drink a bottle of *kvass* at Rosa Klyatskina's. On the eve of Saint John's Day, Anna Ivanovna put on a fete. On the apple trees hung paper lanterns. The musicians from the public garden played. Before the orchard sauntered the entire town. The telegraphist from the station burned Bengal lights, everything was illuminated, and the boys on the street loudly read the inscriptions on fences.

4

Anna Ivanovna and Marya Karlovna were sitting in Frau Anna Rabe's flower garden.

"All evening I had been playing on the physharmonium canticles," Frau Anna was recounting. "Then it got dark completely, and I shut the physharmonium and went to the porch a little to be standing. On the sky there were much stars; I lifted my head and watched. It was being so interesting—I saw a scarf and various crockery, much different pots, saucepans. I was happy, was standing and was laughing. Lizhbetka comes: 'Have you seen Zodelchen?' 'No.' And there you have it, today she was founded past the vegetable garden in the nettles."

"Yes," said Anna Ivanovna, looking at the fence corseted with haricot beans. "Today Zodelchen, tomorrow Elza, by and by . . ." She fell silent and lifted her eyes to the gray sky.

Marya Karlovna sighed and began to nod her head.

"Karlchen loved her so . . . After dinner he goes a little to be looking at his patients, would put on his little hat—he'd got such a little hat with a little green feather. Zodelchen—with him together. I am watering the garden rows, looking on the kitchen. Then suddenly these dog barks—Karlchen is on the corner and waves witt hees little kep . . ."

Frau Anna bowed her head. The guests, lowering their eyes, were silent. From the flowerbed came the smell of gillyflowers. The tea got cold in the three cups . . . A dray began to clatter, came to a halt, everyone lifted their heads. The gate banged, and along the lilac-bordered path Marya Karlovna's husband came running.

"Katerina Alexandrovna's not here? War's been declared. Arrived from the station, and there you have it . . ."

The ladies stood up. "Katerina Alexandrovna is on the hill," said Marya Karlovna, "contemplating her will. Run."

"Your land here is so quiet today, goodness gracious. They came past from the station, went thundering past, and then quiet once again. Over there, some beefy guys are bathing without hollering . . . The road to the palazzo lies beneath the trees like a dead woman . . . You're reminded of an autumn evening: it was growing dark, it was quiet, two narrow leaves were hanging on a slender twig, little cupolas with whitish gilding were reaching toward the gray sky . . ."

"Katerina Alexandrovna, war's been declared!"

Katerina Alexandrovna crossed herself. "Go down, I'll think a bit." After a minute she descended. "Let's go." Dashenka and Hieretiida strode behind. From the orchards came the smell of apples.

Each ate a piece of bread and butter. Katerina Alexandrovna set her coiffure straight and put on a chain. Marya Karlovna smoothed her jacket with the palms of her hands and put white dresses on the little girls. Her husband took Katerina Alexandrovna's arm. "Auntie, you go with him, I'll go with the children—in front of you. Dashenka—up front with the flag. Hieretiida will go behind . . . At Pferdchen's missus's place we'll shout, 'Down with Germany.'" Katerina Alexandrovna said, "God be with us," long faces were made, Hieretiida opened the gate, Marya Karlovna waved her arms, like a precentor in a choir, and they began singing "God keep the tsar" and went out onto the street, overgrown with chamomile.

Gavrilova and her summer tenant had finished cleaning the gooseberries. Gavrilova crossed herself and said, "Well, good luck." They wiped off the hairpins with paper and stuck them in place in their hair. Rinsed their hands and ran down beneath the railroad embankment to bathe. "Boys, clear off!"

It grew dark. The precipice on the other shore was yellow-red, as though the sunset were shining on it.

They had a good swim, and, arms crossed, stood quietly in the dark water. "Heh, wait a bit, what's the story?" The tenant leapt out, pulled on her shirt, and ran off. "War's been declared," she shouted, panting, and began to get dressed. "A bunch of people . . . the excise official with a flute! . . ." Gavrilova alone stood over the water, hurrying, and with her fingers shaking, got tangled in her laces.

Ninon

Mother Olympiada was reading devoutly in a bass voice. The mirrors had been curtained. Arranged around Ninon were the plants that had been dragged from her room: myrtle, laurel, eucalyptus, cypress . . . Yesterday she had not looked good, but today she had swelled up, her wrinkles had stretched out, and everyone was discovering that she had become very striking.

Marie was sitting motionlessly in a corner of the sofa, small, gray-haired, with shaking pink cheeks, holding a scented handkerchief at her little nose.

Tapping with her cane, Barb Sobakina, bony, with a gray mustache and beard, entered and crossed herself before the icons.

"Hello, *matushka* Marya Petrovna," she said in an unnatural, sanctimonious voice. "What sorrow! . . . Recognize me?"

Marie became confused, began blinking, and babbled, "But, of course, of course."

"Good people, evidently, are needed there as well," Barb sang out, crossed herself for a while near Ninon, and whispered to the entire room, "How striking!" and in an affected voice began jabbering, walking toward the sofa.

》 《

"A little piece of lace on her cap! . . . Teach me, *matushka*. Forgive me, I understand that now is not the time, but we so . . ." She bent over and glanced into Marie's eyes, "seldom see one another . . . How is it knit?"

Marie, embarrassed, just looked. Barb stood before her and, leaning on her cane, gazed expectantly.

"Then not here," muttered Marie. "Perhaps, let's go to my room?"

"Seven loops in the air," she explained fussily as they went, moving the curtains aside and jogging the doors. "Into the air . . . A little pillar . . . yes, right here, here, in the trunk, a sample . . ."

A little blue lamp burned by the icons. On the table beneath them two stemless roses were floating in a saucer. Almost inaudible through the several walls Mother Olympiada was mumbling in Slavonic over Ninon's ear. The old women were sitting on a little bench before the opened trunk, fingering pieces of lace, embroidery, examining them in the light, trying them against black, against red, and muttering, "with a wrap . . . checkered . . . a French stitch . . ." Marie cast a glance at the guest, rummaged about, took out a dark polished box, removed a little key on a black lace from over her head, and opened it.

"Barb," she said and gave her a little brown photograph.

"Marie . . ."

》 《

"Barb . . . forty years . . ."

"Marie, you know . . ."

"Barb, it was she . . . In the morning, you'd not even manage to brush your hair, and already she's hissing, 'Beware of her, Marie! She's got dirty tricks on her mind. She'll pull you along by the nose . . .' Blaring, blaring . . . while I . . ."

"That's just what I thought," Barb said, and began to laugh. "As soon as I heard today, I immediately took up my cane and presented myself."

Marie began to titter. "Lying there with her nose sticking up! Swelled up like some drowned man, and everyone's: 'So striking, so striking!' . . . And you, Barb, as well."

"Marie . . . silly . . ."

They softly laughed with their toothless mouths, and with her terrible violet-brown hands Barb tenderly stroked Marie's terrible hands, and with her dim, whitish eyes peered into her dim, whitish eyes.

"You're still just as pretty, Barb . . ."

"And you, Marie . . ."

"You had a little mustache then too and on your cheeks, little fluffs . . . And remember, we were being brought to kiss the cross, you were fixing my button from behind, and I took hold of your fingers . . ."

"Yes . . . Oh, Marie . . ."

"Barb, remember . . ."

It was growing dark. The icon lamp was burning. The roses in the saucer smelled more strongly. Linen was strewn upon the floor before the open trunk. The old women, smiling, moved, were sitting on the bed. Mother Olympiada opened the door and called them to the requiem.

"In a minute," Marie told her. "Go . . . Varenka, let's go, the heck with them."

"Yes, let's go, the heck with them," Barb answered with a happy smile, picking up her cane.

Embracing, they slowly set off down the corridor. "Varenka," Marie said dreamily, "but how much happiness you and I would have had over forty years . . . Hold your nose, Varenka," she added maliciously, opening the door to the living room.

Ninon lay among the three church candlesticks, encircled with the eucalyptuses and laurels she had nurtured in tubs with her own hand—and even more swollen than before.

The guests, making glum faces, spoke of her firm character and about the fact that she had become even more striking: had filled out, grown younger, and become even more striking. Marie nodded her head with dignity, and she wanted to wink, to giggle, stick out her tongue. She gently touched Barb's hand, and Barb, happy, holding back laughter, squeezed her fingers.

Farewell

"Farewell" was first published in the collection *The Portrait* (1931). The translation is based on that text. A longer, quite different variant, with the title "The Aunt" ("*Tyotka*"), was published for the first time in *Raskoldovannyi krug: Vasilii Andreev. Nikolai Barshchev. Leonid Dobychin,* ed. Aleksandr Ageev (Leningrad: Sovetskii pisatel', 1990). It seems to represent one of Dobychin's belated efforts to render his stories more acceptable to the authorities by effacing an earlier version's sarcasm and unflattering portrayal of the new Soviet reality. This later variant lacks most of the present version's evocations of the topsy-turvy post-Revolutionary political situation, in which various political factions, as reflected in the enumeration of different newspapers representing widely divergent points on the political spectrum, still competed. All oppositional voices in Russia were soon thereafter silenced in favor of the Leninist monologue. By the time Dobychin was recasting this material, the days when squat generals could hawk the *New Times* and Cadets (members of the Constitutional Democratic Party) or Mensheviks could toot their causes openly were a distant memory.

The later version is set partly at St. Petersburg's Polytechnic Institute, where Dobychin had been studying during the period in which he sets the story. It focuses more explicitly on the hunger facing the civilian population, as opposed to the sleek, "sated" military men who have commandeered the Institute's cafeteria. Mirra Osipovna in the new variant is a more comic figure who repeats that she comes from Austria and had illegally crossed the border because she expected "something special" in the new Russia. In that version Baumshtein is arrested in the office for accepting bribes. The "bonuses" are not merely "not permitted" by the union but are also protested by the union workers as "degrading to proletarian dignity." Kunst, in the later version, is no longer sexually squeamish, but a tough judge of feminine pulchritude: upon meeting Mirra Osipovna, Kunst's first thought is "You're too old"; upon seeing the maiden Simon, Kunst dismisses her with the words "She's skinny."

3   *The Age (Vek)*   This newspaper, an organ of the liberal Cadet Party, appeared under the name *The Age* only twice, on November 23 and 24 (December 6 and 7 by the Gregorian calendar subsequently adopted in the Soviet Union), 1917. Founded as *Speech (Rech')* in 1906 and closed in 1917, it was periodically revived under various different names (*Dobychin-99*, 459). The appearance here of the newspapers *The Age* and *The Beam* (see below) would seem to place the events portrayed at the beginning of the story in the days just after the October (Bolshevik) Revolution. This appears to conflict with the story's opening sentence, "Winter was drawing to a close."

3   *a nightbird, a pavement nymph*   The Russian terms *"feia"* and *"ulichnaia babochka"* are euphemisms for streetwalker or prostitute, which translate literally as "fairy" and "street butterfly."

3   *Trinity Bridge*   This bridge spans the Neva River in St. Petersburg, bridging the Field of Mars with the Petrograd Quarter.

3-4   *Old stone men stood in faded red-brown niches*   These are probably the statues of classical figures that stand in the decorative niches of the facade of Giacomo Quarenghi's (1744–1817) Hermitage Theater, which faces the Neva River and is linked to the Old Hermitage and the Winter Palace by a covered passage over the Winter Canal.

4   *The Beam (Luch)*   One of the names taken by the Menshevik newspaper, *The Spark (Iskra)*, after it was banned on several occasions in 1917. With this name, the paper came out only two or three times in all, on November 19, 20, and possibly 21 (that is, December 2, 3, and possibly 4 of the Gregorian calendar), 1917 (*Dobychin-99*, 459).

4   *New Times (Novoe vremya)*   An influential St. Petersburg news-paper (1865–1917) famous for its conservative views, it was owned and edited for most of its existence by the publishing magnate and journalist Alexei Suvorin (1834–1912).

4   *distribution (vydacha)*   A Soviet institution of privilege, later known as a "*zakaz*" or "*nabor*," wherein deficit goods were handed out to government workers.

4   *"Perhaps Simòn would be more correct"*   Ivan Ilyich shifts the stress in his pronunciation of Simon from the first to the second syllable.

6   *vobla*   A type of fish—Caspian roach—usually preserved in salt. A favorite Russian snack, it has a powerful odor and is accompanied by beer.

7   *Black River*   A small river in the outskirts of St. Petersburg, famed as the site of Alexander Pushkin's fatal duel in 1837.

8   *Max Stirner*   Pen name of Johann Kaspar Schmidt (1806–1856), German young Hegelian, author of *The Ego and His Own* (1845), a treatise in defense of philosophic egoism and social anarchism. Stirner's individualism—by definition antagonistic to the philo-sophical underpinnings of Communism—became something of a red flag to Soviet ideological bulls. *The Great Soviet Encyclopedia* identifies the cause of Stirner's appearance in Dobychin's early Soviet milieu when it observes: "K. Marx and F. Engels, in their *The German Ideology [. . .]*, offered a devastating critique of Stirner's subjective idealism and his petit bourgeois individualism and anarchism; they demonstrated the utter groundlessness of his criticism of communism" (English translation [London, 1982] of the Third Edition [Moscow, 1978], vol. 29, 696).

8   *Courland Province*   The semi-independent Duchy of Courland, set along the Baltic coast and historically part of Latvia, was annexed in 1795 by Russia and became a province in Soviet times.

8   *Filyanka*   The Finnish Railroad (*Dobychin-99*, 459). This is pre-
     sumably a local nickname for this rail line. In "Timofeyev," a little
     sketch that adumbrates some of the characters and events of
     "Farewell," Dobychin has Kunst's predecessor, Timofeyev, sitting
     on the porch with his landlady one evening, when they hear a dis-
     tant whistle and she sighs and whispers, "Filyanka." When Timo-
     feyev asks for an explanation, she replies, "The Filyanka railroad."

Kozlova

Written in 1923, "Kozlova" was first published in *Leningrad*, no. 9 (48)
1925. The translation is based on the text in *The Portrait* (1931). The
name "Kozlova" might be translated literally as "Miss Goat." In his letters Dobychin frequently announced an intention to write works of substantial length, of a size that would be attractive to publishers, but his
efforts almost invariably succumbed to an aesthetic disposition to reduce
stories to their most densely crystallized essence. Of "Kozlova," which in
his preconception was to have become a work of considerable length, he
writes to his editor, M. L. Slonimsky, on June 13, 1925: "I am sending the
goat [Dobychin referred to his stories by just about anything other than
their actual titles]. I boasted, boasted, but it came out shorter than a spar-
row's nose" (*Dobychin-99*, 273).

9   *Forty-eight Soviet office workers were singing in the choir*   The paral-
     lel enumerations ("three church chandeliers," "forty-eight Soviet
     office workers") effectively link the two, the inanimate with the ani-
     mate, comically reducing the latter. The very presence of all these
     Soviet office workers singing in church is itself comical: all good
     Soviet citizens should have denounced the backward superstitions
     of religion in favor of materialistic atheism. After all, they and their
     employer, the Soviet state, are the very "enemies" whom the
     "newly arrived" preacher is promising God will scatter. Why a
     "newly arrived" preacher? Is it because he, a neophyte, does not yet
     know the dangers of calling divine damnation down upon Soviet
     power? The electricity burning in the church chandeliers is another
     curious detail. Why electricity instead of the usual candles? Is
     Dobychin winking at the reader, conjuring up Lenin's dictum that

"Communism equals Soviet power plus the electrification of the entire nation"? The electrification of the nation's churches was the last thing Lenin had in mind.

9 *God would rise again and his enemies would be scattered* An allusion to the opening words of the sixty-seventh psalm of David in the Russian Bible (in the King James English text, it is the sixty-eighth psalm).

9 *Karl Liebknecht and Rosa Luxemburg School* The school is named for Karl Liebknecht (1871–1919) and Rosa Luxemburg (1871–1919), the two founders of the Marxist Spartacus Party, forerunner to the German Communist Party, who were arrested and murdered after the Spartacist uprising in 1919. Innumerable Soviet streets, factories, parks, and schools were named in their honor.

10 *Madame de Thèbes* Born Anne-Victorine Savigny, Madame de Thèbes (1844–1916) was a Parisian chiromancer and soothsayer who was launched on her career by Alexandre Dumas *fils* in 1886 and became a star of French salons between 1890 and 1905. She published almanacs with sage advice and books of predictions that, in the view of her fans, frequently were borne out. Her 1912 collection, in which she predicted that 1914 would be marked by the beginning of "great events," was republished in Russia in 1914 along with a booklet entitled "What Does Madame de Thèbes Say about Current Affairs?" (*Dobychin-99*, 460, with my corrections, and Nicole Edelman, *Voyantes, guerisseuses et visionnaires en France*, 1785–1914 [Paris: Bibliothèque Albin Michel, 1995], 51).

10 *The Cornfield (Niva)* A popular, middlebrow, illustrated journal (1870–1918) of current affairs, which featured literary supplements.

11 *the Winter Palace . . . the Admiralty* The two most prominent architectural structures in St. Petersburg (Leningrad), the Winter Palace (which after the Revolution became the Hermitage Museum) and its massive yellow neighbor on the banks of the

Neva, the Admiralty, formed the nucleus of Peter the Great's (1672–1725) original city.

11   *Saint Kuksha*   A twelfth-century monk, bishop, and anchorite, originally from the Pechersky (Cave) Monastery in Kiev, Kuksha was famous as a miracle worker and for his conversions of pagan tribes. He was eventually tortured and beheaded by pagans. His relics were transferred from Kiev to the city of Bryansk—where Dobychin was later to reside—in 1903. His memory is observed on August 27.

11   *Moussiour*   This represents Suslova's unsuccessful pronunciation of the French "*monsieur*" (in Russian, it is "*mus'iu,*" rather than the standard "*mos'e*").

11   "*Venezia e Napoli*"   Italian, "Venice and Naples." This is perhaps the name of a perfume sold in the local cooperative store that burned.

12   "*Won't be tormented long*"   Perhaps this is because Kozlova has had a vision of Saint Kuksha and takes this to be a good sign. Another possibility derives from the Russian folk belief that a full bucket (in this case, the bishop's bucket of slops) is a sign of good luck.

12   *Curzon (Kerzon in the Russian text)*   George Nathaniel Curzon, First Marquess of Kedleston (1859–1925), English statesman and diplomat. While a man of many accomplishments, Russians recall him principally as the British Foreign Secretary (1919–24) who helped plan the "intervention" by Western powers against Soviet Russia in the early 1920s. V. S. Bakhtin (*Dobychin-99,* 461) notes that during the well-organized demonstrations in which Curzon was hung in effigy, a popular slogan was "*Lordu-v mordu,*" which, without the Russian's jingly rhyme, translates roughly as "right in the lord's ugly mug."

12   "*England's joined the war*"   Curzon's 1923 ultimatum that he would break off diplomatic relations with Soviet Russia if it did not

cease its Comintern propaganda and its assistance of national liberation movements in the East doubtless led to rumors that a new "intervention" by Western powers was in the offing (*Dobychin-99*, 461).

13   *John the Warrior*   Fourth-century Christian martyr whose memory is observed on July 30.

13   *finkotrud union*   The Union of Financial and Control Affairs Workers (*Soiuz rabotnikov finansovogo i kontrol'nogo dela RSFSR*), an institution that existed from June 1919 until 1920, when it was included within the structure of the amalgamated Union of Workers of Soviet and Social Institutions and Enterprises (*Soiuz rabotnikov sovetskikh i obshchestvennykh uchrezhdenii i predpriiatii*). From June 22 until October 1925 Dobychin was employed in the *Gubprofsovet*, the Provincial Council (Soviet) of Professional Unions, and was quite familiar with the structures of Soviet professional organizations, to which he makes frequent reference in his fiction (*Dobychin-99*, 461–62).

14   *the regeneration of icons (obnovlenie ikon)*   V. S. Bakhtin (*Dobychin-99*, 462) defines this as: "The miraculous alteration of the external appearance of an icon, explained as the intervention of Divine Providence" (editor's translation). In *Shurka's Kin* (probably completed in 1936; first published in 1993), Dobychin's last work of fiction, he describes one such miraculous "regeneration" when a "new" icon is discovered to have appeared in a cemetery on the cross over the remains of a young boy, apparently replacing an earlier icon or rejuvenating an older one. This discovery creates a sensation in the village in which it occurs and in surrounding towns.

15   *November 7*   The day on which the October (Bolshevik) Revolution was celebrated in the Soviet Union.

16   *the red-brown palace*   The Winter Palace was painted red and brown before the Revolution.

16　　*Here had taught Monsieur Poincaré*　　Like James Joyce and Vladimir Nabokov, Dobychin frequently contrives circular narrative structures. In the case of Dobychin, these circles are ironical, describing "journeys" that double back on themselves, headed nowhere. "Kozlova" begins with the electricity in the church chandeliers and ends with the electricity of the streetlights. It opens with a reminiscence of Monsieur Poincaré and closes with one. It commences with the dull comfort of friendship with Suslova and, following a disruption, concludes with Suslova's dull, comforting friendship. It starts with Karl Liebknecht and Rosa Luxemburg and ends with them.

Encounters with Lise

"Encounters with Lise" *("Vstrechi s Liz")* was first published in *Russkii sovremennik*, no. 4 (1924). The translation is based on the text in *The Portrait* (1931).

19　　*"Rise, accursed"*　　The opening words of "The International" (*"L'Internationale"*), then the Soviet national anthem.

19　　*"Down with Household Breeding Grounds!"*　　The Russian is a play on words: *"Doloi domashnie! Ochagi!" "Domashnii ochag"* means "hearth and home," but *"ochag"* is also a place bacteria and other organisms lodge and multiply—a "nidus," a nest or breeding ground. In the early 1920s certain Bolshevik utopians dreamed of doing away with such "bourgeois" institutions as the family kitchen (to be replaced by communal dining facilities) and even with the family itself as a relevant social unit. This slogan encourages the destruction of the conditions that lead to disease, one of which ostensibly was the traditional family hearth and home.

19　　*Mercedes of Castile*　　A romantic adventure novel (1840) by James Fenimore Cooper (1789–1851) concerning Christopher Columbus's discovery of America.

19   *Pisemsky (Alexei Feofilaktovich)*   A popular writer (1820–81) of realistic stories, novels, and plays portraying contemporary Russia. His best-known work is the novel *A Thousand Souls* (1859).

20   *"Down with Rumania"* Relations between Rumania and the Soviet Union had been strained since 1918, when Bessarabia detached itself from Russian control and joined with Rumania, a union the Soviet regime did not recognize. In 1924, the year this story was written, the Rumanian government outlawed the Rumanian Communist Party.

21   *the gubsoyuz* An acronym for provincial union (*gubernskii soiuz*).

21   *The Torture Garden* A novel by French radical anarchist Octave Mirbeau (1848–1917), *The Torture Garden* (1899) is a disturbing social satire, widely considered indecent and decadent. It takes erotic sadomasochism as its metaphor for Western civilization's cruelties and hypocrisies. Riva makes a comical, though probably unconscious association between the Marx and Engels Garden in contemporary Soviet Russia and Mirbeau's "Torture Garden," an imaginary floral paradise in China where prisoners are tortured to death for the aesthetic and sexual pleasure of spectators.

21   *reaching the end of "Blancmange"* Blancmange, a French dish, is a gelatin made from milk, almonds, and sweetener. V. S. Bakhtin (*Dobychin-99*, 463) concludes: "Evidently, Kukin is reading a cookbook." Given Kukin's next remark—"Ah," he sighed, "the old days won't be coming back"—Kukin is, perhaps, reading a pre-Revolutionary cookbook, which describes the French cuisine that Kukin suspects will not be returning to a Russia under Soviet rule. Shortly thereafter, we find the Kukins and Zolotukhina eating *kisel'*, a sort of Russian *blancmange*.

22   *Saint Euplus* According to V. S. Bakhtin, this Russian church ("*Sviatoi Evpl [Eupl]*," or Saint Euplus) is named for Archdeacon Euplus (Euplius), a Christian martyr of the fourth century whose memory is observed on August 11 (*Dobychin-99*, 463).

23   *Peasant men . . . thronged (tolpilis')*   Note the equation of the wedding guests "thronging" at the end of the third part of the story and these peasants and bathers "thronging" around the corpse of the drowned Lise, whose funeral also will be held at Saint Euplus. Likewise, the smell of powder that attends the wedding contrasts with the smell of human decomposition that signals Lise's impending funeral.

23   *"no Marxist approach whatsoever!"*   These words were excised in the *Russkii sovremennik* publication. In a letter to Kornei Chukovsky, Dobychin complains: "You know, the part of the omitted text ("Encounters with Lise") that grieves me most is that about 'no Marxist approach whatsoever.' Half of Fishkina has fallen off with that. Allow me to make You a little present—a discussion of 'freedom of the press' cut out of the newspaper *Trud*." Dobychin refers to an article entitled "The Bourgeoisie's Freedom of the Press" that appeared in that Soviet newspaper on January 16, 1925. The words were restored in the collection *Encounters with Lise* (1927) (*Dobychin-99, 507*).

23   *kisel'*   Kissel, a kind of Russian *blancmange* (see note above), is a gelatin dessert made of fruit and potato starch and served with milk.

23   *"In the companies"*   "The companies" (*roty*) was the unofficial name given to the grid of streets in St. Petersburg situated in the area of the Izmailovsky Guards Regiment barracks and the intersecting Izmailovsky Prospect. The first, northernmost street was called "First Izmailovsky Company" (*Pervaya Izmailovskaya Rota*), and so on. In 1923 these streets were renamed for the Red Army (*Krasnoarmeiskie*), as was Izmailovsky Prospect.

24   *"God, Tsar"*   "God Save the Tsar" ("*Bozhe, tsaria khrani*") was the official anthem of the Russian Empire. Zolotukhina, loyal to the vanished Empire, is roused to make this observation when she hears the soldiers singing the new, Soviet anthem, and because Saint Euplus reminds her of Petersburg.

Lidiya

Written in 1925, "Lidiya" was first published, together with "Yerygin" and "Sorokina" (later called "Dorian Gray") in the almanac *Kovsh*, book 4 (1926). The translation is based on the text in *The Portrait* (1931).

Dobychin indicated in a personal letter that he had taken the goat's name, "Lidiya," from Lidiya Seifullina (1889–1954), a major Soviet writer to whom he referred in his letters in an ironical, if not mocking tone. Seifullina's short novel, *Virineya* (1924), is seen on the "recommended" table at the public library in "The Portrait." In letters to Kornei Chukovsky (#8 and 19, *Dobychin-99*), however, Dobychin asserted that *Virineya* is not writing, but "lisping" (*siusiukan'e*).

25   *"Stream on, my pioneer song!"* Lines from a popular song of the 1920s, "Baklazhechka" (*Dobychin-99*, 463). The Pioneers were a group the Soviet Communist Party organized for children ages ten through sixteen.

26   *her sweated flanks* Details in this story create peculiar patterns. One comprises a blurring of boundaries between human and animal, living and dead, male and female. Zaitseva's "flanks" are echoed by the goat's, and her white mustaches by the goat's white eyelashes. Her mustaches also recall those of Barb in "Ninon." People do not "walk" or "run," but "hop," "spring," and "leap," all verbs that derive from a root—*skok/skak* (*poskakala, vyskochila, soskochili, uskochila*)—that is more frequently associated with animals. Cows "trudge" (*plelis'*), a goat is "pompous" (*vazhnaia*), and sparrows "scream" (*krichali*). Little boys "pour" or "spill out" onto the road, like sand or grain. Zaitseva's attraction to the Youth Leader is implicitly linked with the need to get the nanny goat "Lidiya" a billy for mating. She apparently finds an appropriate billy at the end, and it turns out to belong to the Youth Group, and is being driven by the Youth Leader himself. People pack a picnic and visit a drowned man, as if he were giving a party, and when the corpse "surfaces," the verb employed—*"vyplyt'"*—has as its primary definition the alive-sounding "swim out." Lidiya, the eponymous goat, used to be named "Georgie," but had been renamed

because Georgie was "not a woman's name" (which recalls Dobychin's *Shurka's Kin* [1936, first published in 1993] in which a bitch is named "Jack").

26   *receiving the icon*   Svistunikha has arranged for the local clergy to conduct a special religious service in her home on this Orthodox holiday.

26   *Deniken*   Anton Pavlovich (1872–1947), a Russian general who commanded the anti-Bolshevik forces in southern Russia during the Civil War (1918–20).

27   *SR Party*   The Socialist Revolutionary Party. This would be a pre-Bolshevik Revolutionary poster from 1917, now seven or eight years old, for elections to the short-lived Constituent Assembly.

27   *Comrade Figatner*   There was a prominent "old Bolshevik," Iurii Petrovich Figatner (1889–1938), who eventually fell victim to Stalin's purges. He was a member of the presidium of the All-Union Central Council of Professional Unions at a time when Dobychin was employed by the Provincial Council of Professional Unions. Dobychin may have been drawn to the comic juxtaposition of the weighty "Comrade" with the colloquial "*fig*" (a Russian gesture of derision or contempt, similar to the English "cocking a snook") in "Figatner."

28   *drachyona*   Also *drochena*, a flat cake baked from a mixture of eggs, milk, and flour or potato.

28   *"Theirs?"*   By "theirs" (*ikhnii*) Zaitseva presumably refers to the youth organization of which the young man is leader, and to which the goat belongs. Zaitseva is likely beaming because her interest in finding a billy for her nanny goat coincides with her interest in this youth.

Savkina

Written in 1924, "Savkina" was first published in *Leningrad*, no. 23 (62), June 27, 1925. The translation is based on the text in *The Portrait* (1931). In a letter of May 11, 1925, to M. L. Slonimsky, Dobychin writes that his "Savkina" came out "vapid" (*pustoporozhniaia*) because it is "bereft of politics" (*bez politiki*) (*Dobychin-99*, 273). This statement is deliberately coy, given that the Bolshevik Revolution had politicized all aspects of Soviet life and that, as a string of comical snapshots of Soviet society, "Savkina" is packed with "politics": conflict between the church and the Communist Party over religious rites; wall newspapers that attack a citizen for the mere fact that a relative had kept a shop before the Revolution; derogation of a certain style of dressing as "bourgeois"; public denunciation of a teacher for her fraternization with a priest. The notion that Dobychin was writing a literature bereft of politics is one that he asserts in letters numerous times, but it is undermined by his playful references in other letters to the "Dear Chiefs" and whether they will disallow what he has written.

Despite the story's poker-faced political irony, "Savkina" is best characterized as an ironical love story, or as a love story parody. In this, it is structured identically to "The Portrait." In both stories the young protagonist briefly glimpses an unknown cavalier, and then for the remainder of the story dreams of him, only to rediscover him in an ironical context at the story's conclusion. Dobychin's stories often take the form of parodies or inversions of the traditional trajectories of love stories. In addition to "The Portrait" and "Savkina," Dobychin's "love" stories include "Encounters with Lise," "Dorian Gray," "Palmistry," "Yerygin," "The Nurse," "As You Wish"—in which an impoverished lady loses one goat (animal) and is forced to take on another one (human)—and perhaps "Konopatchikova," "The Medass," and "Tea" as well. The romantic paradigm to which characters such as Savkina and Sorokina ("Dorian Gray") aspire is outlined in "Savkina" in the cinematic drama of "Miss May" and "clubman Baybl." In this regard, the story "Ninon" stands apart. While darkly humorous in its treatment of the deceased, it is also a love story with a happy, if bittersweet ending, and remains, for all its idiosyncrasy, Dobychin's most traditional story.

30   *"They's offendered"*   Kukel's substandard Russian adds a superfluous consonant to the word "offended" (*obizhdaiutsia*).

30   *"The Dnieper is lovely in calm weather"*   The initial words of the panegyrical digression that opens Chapter Ten of Nikolai Gogol's (1809–52) story "A Terrible Vengeance" (1832).

30   *"at their church"*   "Their" (*ikhnii*) refers to Roman Catholics here; the word used for church here ("*kostyol*") refers only to Polish Roman Catholic churches, just as the word for priest, "*ksyondz*," used by Kukel earlier, refers to a Roman Catholic priest, rather than a Russian Orthodox or Protestant cleric.

32   *Mari-Ivana*   How one would refer casually in spoken Russian to someone named "Marya Ivanovna."

32   *Narobraz*   An acronym for *Otdel narodnogo obrazovaniia*, or Department of National—or Popular—Education, the government department to which Pavlushenka is directing his denunciation of the "Frenchwoman" (presumably merely a teacher of French) for her fraternization with the Catholic priest.

33   *"all the Communards"*   A variant of a line from an anonymous song of the Russian Civil War (1918–20), "The Execution of the Communards" (*Dobychin-99*, 464), it refers to the 1871 Commune of Paris, the insurrectionary government established after France's defeat in the Franco-Prussian War (1870–71). When the leadership of the Commune refused to surrender to the regular armies, a massacre of some twenty thousand Communards ensued in the week of May 21–28. Marx's, and later Lenin's, interpretation of the events of 1871 as the first proletarian uprising and dictatorship elevated the Commune to mythical stature in the Soviet version of history.

Yerygin

Written in 1924, "Yerygin" was first published in *Kovsh*, book 4 (1926). Excepting corrections of what appear to be errors, the translation is based on the text from *Material* (*Dobychin-99,* 380–84), where Dobychin highlights Yerygin's fictional creations with double indentation.

In an effort to soften the satire of "Yerygin" and accentuate its politically "correct" moments, Dobychin outlined to his editor, M. L. Slonimsky, a number of possible emendations. None of these was made, but they adumbrate where Dobychin perceived dangers to lie:

5 April [1925].

Dear M. L. Let's try to make several changes in Yerygin.

1. At the end of the first chapter the last word in place of "RCP(b)"—simply "RCP."

If even this isn't enough, then maybe: "The *nachdiv* went away, carrying with him the memory of the upstanding non-Party woman who had saved his life."

2. In the second chapter depict the foreigners' speeches thus: "Deceived by the bourgeois press, they had never expected what they'd happened to see."

3. Redo the end of the fourth chapter, beginning from "listens to the trills and drinks tea" and put it thus: " . . . tea. 'Comrade Leningradov,' Gadova turns around, 'I cannot remain silent any longer.' And reveals about the bishop. 'You knew and didn't inform,' says Comrade Generalov <so!> and his love was as if it had never existed. Once again he is hard as a rock face, and henceforward he'll be lured into bourgeois nets no more."

If it's necessary, you can remove the phrases "The company advances . . ." and "A jobless person created a scandal . . ." in the third chapter, but it's better to leave them, without them it will be bobtailed.

Please try to arrange this: perhaps then it'll get past [the censor]. It seems to me that the main concern is in these places. It's also possible to omit that the mother, returning from the club, was spitting curses: but it'd be better to leave it (it's in the fourth chapter).

Your L. Dobychin

Dobychin-99, 270–71

34   *Its hair made traces in the sand*   Evidence that Dobychin's subtlety may have escaped even his best contemporary readers arises in a letter he wrote to Slonimsky in which he reports:

[Kornei] Chukovsky writes that he would begin Yerygin with the second paragraph. The first paragraph is necessary. It's there that there are the traces in the sand from the hair, in the fourth chapter there are traces on the snow from the hay, whence it is written "something came back." Please don't throw out the first paragraph.

Yerygin's epiphany, in which all of the random, mundane events and fantasies revolving in his brain are transfigured into a coherent structure and suffused with meaning, is precipitated by the perception of the similar traces in sand and snow. It anticipates Vladimir Nabokov's use of a nearly identical structure in his 1935 story "Torpid Smoke" for the evocation of a flash of literary inspiration. Given what we discover to be the theme of Yerygin's "art," however, this story constitutes less a "Portrait of the Artist as a Young Man" than a parody of such, a "Portrait of the Soviet Literary Hack as a Young Fool."

Yerygin's creative transmutation of mundane experience and fantasy links him with the child, Lyoshka, in "The Sailor," another protoartist figure and exploiter of metaphoric imagination. Just as Lyoshka defines the sailor's inflated muscles by comparing them with the bread he had seen earlier in the day and defines clouds by their resemblance to heaps of linen, so Yerygin, consciously or not, transfigures his friends Zakharov and Vakhrameyev, who are initially described as "Corpulent . . . wearing striped cotton jerseys," into the "sturdy sailors" of his fiction. Likewise, Yerygin's comparison of the moon to a steamship window derives from his fantasy about the foreign lady peeping out of a steamship window.

34   *Metric tables were suspended on stalls*   The metric system was adopted in the Soviet Union in the first years following the 1917 Revolution.

34   *Krasnaya Presnya*   This is a slightly parodic example of the early Soviet trend of giving children revolutionary names such as "Vladlen"—from the amalgamation of "Vladimir" and "Lenin." Others named their children after the brand of furnaces ("Martena") used in the new factory works. In this case, Krasnaya

Presnya is the name of a working-class neighborhood in Moscow renowned for its revolutionary spirit.

35   *rapprochement with the Red Army*   "One of a series of ubiquitous political slogans of the 1920s that proposed rapprochement between the populace (that is, institutions, enterprises, factories) and the army via personal contacts, exchanges of amateur talent shows, material assistance. There also existed slogans about the rapprochement [*smychka*] of city and countryside, worker and peasant. A Society of Cultural Rapprochement was created, 'Rapprochement' cigarettes were marketed, and a newspaper of that name was published" (V. S. Bakhtin, *Dobychin-99*, 465; editor's translation).

36   *nachdiv*   An acronym for *nachal'nik divizii* ("division commander").

36   *izba*   A Russian peasant's hut.

36   *RCP(b)*   *Rossiiskaia Kommunisticheskaia partiia (bol'shevikov)*, the Russian Communist Party (of Bolsheviks).

36   *Madmazelle Wuntsch*   "Madmazelle" is a rendering of the spelling in the Russian text (*Madmazel'*), which reflects the locals' unsuccessful attempt to pronounce French. While there are antecedents for transliterating the French form of address as it is generally pronounced (usually "*mamzel'*"), the standard literary rendering of "mademoiselle" in Russian is either the phonetically exact "*mademuazel'*," the less pedantic "*madmuazel'*," or else the immediate use of the Latin lettered word. When, for example, a real French character, such as Monsieur Poincaré in "Kozlova," pronounces the word, it is rendered "madmuazel'."

38   *The little gold sphere on the green cupola of the "October" Club glittered*   The October Club is housed in a former church (a fate shared by thousands of churches in Russia after the Revolution).

39   *"Narpit"*   An acronym for an early Soviet organization charged
with opening a network of public cafeterias: *Narodnoe pitanie,*
National Nutrition.

39   *Dawes Plan*   In 1924 a committee headed by Charles G. Dawes
(1865–1951) submitted its report to the Allied Reparations Commission. It called for the reduction of Germany's reparations after
World War I and the stabilization of German finances.

40   *social traitors*   This was the epithet the Soviet press affixed to the
German Social Democrats, Philipp Scheidemann (1865–1939) and
Gustav Noske (1868–1946), who opposed revolution in Germany
(*Dobychin-99,* 466).

40   *On the seventh and eighth they had a good time*   November 7 is the
day the Soviet people celebrated the October (Bolshevik) Revolution.

40   *Nepwoman*   The devastating effects of the Civil War (1918–20) on
Russia's economy obliged Lenin to initiate his New Economic Policy (NEP) in 1921, loosening restrictions on private trade. Those
who took advantage of the new opportunities were cast in the popular imagination as "Nepmen" (and "Nepwomen")—sinister,
greedy capitalist caricatures who enriched themselves by exploiting
others and manipulating economic structures.

40   *Intelligentka Gadova*   Russia's traditionally liberal intelligentsia
was regarded with suspicion by the revolutionary proletariat.
"Gadova" might be translated literally as "Miss Reptile" or "Miss
Vile." The final plot concocted by Yerygin, about Comrade
Leningradov and Gadova, parodies the journalist Sergei Ingulov's
(1893–?) famous revolutionary romance about the "Girl from the
(Bolshevik) Party School" (1921).

Konopatchikova

Written in 1926, "Konopatchikova" was first published in *Encounters with Lise* (1927). The translation is based on the text in *The Portrait* (1931).

Some of the names in Dobychin's stories may strike the Russian ear as ridiculous. Thus, "Konopatchikova" might be rendered literally as "Miss Caulker." Other comic names include Kuroedova ("Miss Chicken Eater"), Vdovkin ("Mr. Little Widow"), and Beryozynkina ("Miss Nice Little Birch Tree").

41   *"Ilyich and the Specialists"*   Ilyich is Vladimir Lenin's patronymic. This is a rather cloying form of reference to the Revolutionary leader that became widespread in Soviet times. The role to be played by "specialists"—engineers, agronomists, economists, industrial managers—in the building of the first Communist state was a controversial issue during the first decade of Soviet rule. By definition trained experts were not members of the proletariat or peasantry, and hence foreign or "bourgeois" specialists were to be tolerated as an unfortunate necessity until members of the new ruling class attained the requisite skills, discipline, and probity to play leading technical roles in their culture.

41   *Cultural Commission*   In the Russian, "Cultural Commission" is rendered as a one-word acronym, *"kul'tkomissiia."*

41   *Women's Section rep*   In Russian this is another Soviet acronym, *"zhenotdelka."* Malkina represents the section of a Communist Party organization that conducts agitation—political work—among women workers and peasants.

43   *"L'egleez dez Envaleed," "Statyu de Anree Katr"*   These words render the Russian transliteration of the French *"L'église des Invalides"* and *"Statue d'Henri IV."*

43   *Kapitannichikha*   The widow of the previously mentioned Kapitannikov.

43   *"And why'd you have all this stuff made," she lamented*   "Dobychin is rather precisely reproducing, if also partly parodying, Russian folk keening, into the traditional form of which (addressing the dead as one would the living) details of everyday life enter organically" (*Dobychin-99*, 467; editor's translation).

43   *Madmazelles* See note to Madmazelle Wuntsch under "Yerygin."

45   *"Middle" peasants* The Russian social and economic classification of the peasantry divided them into *kulaki* (kulaks, those economically best-off); *serednyaki* (middle peasants, those of average means); and *bednyaki* (the poorest peasants). A middle peasant would possess means sufficient for working his own land only, and not for purchasing another's labor.

46   *rabkor* The Soviet acronym for *rabochii korrespondent* ("worker correspondent").

47   *The Cornfield (Niva)* See note to *The Cornfield* under "Kozlova."

Dorian Gray

Written in 1925, "Dorian Gray" was first published in the almanac *Kovsh*, book 4 (1926), under the title "Sorokina." It also appeared as "Sorokina" in the collection *Encounters with Lise* (1927) before becoming "Dorian Gray" in *The Portrait* (1931). In the unpublished collection, *Material*, Dobychin shortened the title to "Dorian." The translation is based on the text in *The Portrait*.

Dorian Gray is the central character in Oscar Wilde's (1854–1900) novel *The Picture of Dorian Gray* (1891).

In a letter of September 9, 1925, to M. L. Slonimsky, Dobychin writes: "I'll send You Sorokina when I've rewritten her, and I'll ask You to read her because I myself can't understand anything in her and don't know whether there can be such a story. There's not a half-kopeck's worth of politics in her, there are Latin words in Russian letters. There's everything—about love affairs* (*That's because I love Seifullina)."

A week later he sent Slonimsky the manuscript, writing: "I can't understand it myself. It seems all the adornments aren't bad at all, but everything all together is—something confectionery, a 'coiffeur Wladislas and Gennady'" (*Dobychin*-99, 276–77). Five years later, when Dobychin created a fictional "coiffeur" in the story "Palmistry," he appropriately dubbed him "Ladislas."

48   *Law Defender Ivanov*   The Russian word "*pravozastupnik*" could be translated as "lawyer," and literally means "defender of the law." It refers, however, to a government post that existed under that name only in the first post-Revolutionary years (1918–22), and embraced both public prosecutors and public defenders.

49   *Cahors*   A wine, once very popular in Russia, from the region of Cahors, capital of the Lot department, in southwestern France.

51   *Sun Yat-sen*   Chinese revolutionary leader and national hero (1866–1925), he was hailed as the "pioneer of the revolution." Leader of the Chinese Nationalist Party, he entered into an agreement with the Soviet Union in 1923 that led to an alliance with the Chinese Communist Party.

51   *the waltz "Diana"*   "Diane, Séléné," music by Gabriel Fauré (1845–1924), lyrics by Jean de la Ville de Mirmont (1886–1914).

51   *"de in jus vocando, de actionue danda"*   Latin, "to act, relying on the law."

52   *Jimmie Higgins*   A novel (1919) by the American socialist Upton Sinclair (1878–1968) about a rank-and-file American Communist Party member.

52   *"In America advertisements are written on clouds . . ."* They dreamed   See the conclusion of "Tea," where the doctor also describes the putative miracles of life in America. To Dobychin's provincials, "America" represents the exotic and unobtainable and evokes that oppressive sense that "life is elsewhere." But it also represents, par-

adoxically, the radiant, ultramodern future promised by the Revolution, when Communism will enable Russia to outstrip the West. Other glimpses of the romantic, the exotic, and the radiant future are embodied in such tropes as *Dorian Gray* and *Jimmie Higgins,* the waltz "Diana," the Law Defender's Latin and thoughts of Italy, the tapir in "Geography," the Cracovienne, and the Cahors and Madeira.

"Dorian Gray" counterbalances the romantic, the exotic, and the radiant future with the banality and vulgarity of provincial life and the remorseless passage of time. The events of the story cover more than half a year, from Lent, when Sorokina sneaks into church for Easter service and birds are building nests (as Sorokina would like to do with Vanya); through summer and its concerts in the park and flowering potatoes; on to autumn, when the gossamer takes flight; and finally to approaching winter, as the dogs start barking "winter style." With the coming of winter, Sorokina's and Millionshchikova's hopes for romance fade. In the face of philistinism, banality, and drunken cavaliers who dance with one another, not with the aging maidens, Sorokina and Millionshchikova already recall with sadness the previous spring, when they still entertained hopes. Time ticks away, and people go on playing patience, sewing, collecting recipes for shoe polish, and listening to the same dull stories again and again, like characters in a Chekhov play.

The ironical theme of "remembering" with nostalgia or regret is pervasive in Dobychin's works, from the Law Defender recalling university days here and Kukin remembering the same in "Encounters with Lise," to the child protagonist prematurely learning the practice of "recalling childhood" in *The Town of N* (1935).

52   *"They say I'm a tramp . . . but I don't even know the roads"*   This play on words is either a silly joke or a pathetic plaint, depending on whether Osipikha intends to be funny or is deeply innocent. *"Guliaka,"* the Russian word translated here as "tramp," more accurately translates as "reveler," "dissipater," or "idler," and is related to the verb *"guliat',"* which primarily means "to stroll," but which colloquially may denote carousing, idling, or "going with"

someone in the sense of "having sex." By defending herself as someone who doesn't even know the roads ("*i dorog ne znaiu*"), Osipikha interprets the accusation against her as merely a reference to her strolling about aimlessly, like a tramp.

52   *presented the newspaper*   Dobychin's use of the verb "*predlozhit'*," which normally translates as "to offer" or "suggest," is idiosyncratic, suggesting that the greenish old man is not merely reading the newspaper—probably one posted on a wall—but is also propounding its ideas to an audience.

52   *the Septentriones*   One name given to the seven brightest stars in the constellation Ursa Major ("The Great Bear").

The Nurse

"The Nurse" ("*Sidelka*") was first published in *Novaia Rossiia*, no. 2 (1926). The translation is based on the text in *The Portrait* (1931).

For his unpublished 1933 collection, *Material*, Dobychin revised "The Nurse," softening its satirical sting in the hope of rendering it republishable in Stalinist times. The first of three major excisions comprises the fragment of the speech delivered at the unveiling of the monument: "Comrade Gusev brought to a near-resolution the tasks confronting the Party." V. S. Bakhtin (*Dobychin-99*, 470) suggests that this alludes to a famous line in an article by Lenin. This is followed by the removal of the little survey of the town square: "They turned this way and that. Behind was the cemetery, to the right—reformatory, in front—barracks." This panorama recalls the opening of Anton Chekhov's "The Steppe" (1888), in which a bleak microcosm of provincial Russian society is glimpsed in the institutions that the protagonist passes as he leaves town. In the present instance, however, the microcosm represented is that of provincial Soviet society, and it is still defined by barracks, prisons, and graveyards. The irony of Dobychin's original version springs from the juxtaposition of these two excised passages, which implicitly links the official's words regarding "near-resolution" of the "tasks confronting the Party" with the survey of the cemetery, reformatory, and barracks, and suggests that a

Soviet world defined by military presence, prisons, and death is precisely the resolution of the Party's tasks.

The third excision concerns the funeral procession of "Syomkina the suicide, expelled for instability," her girlfriend's howling, and Mishka's praise: "Disciplined . . . , not taking part in the procession." This Dobychin replaced with a passage that is politically correct, but little else:

> Old lady Zheleznova was being buried in the way of the church. Religious banners rocked slightly as they went, and voices sang softly, blowing in the wind.
>
> "Religious prejudice," Mishka Dobrokhim came up and touched Mukhin's elbow. "I never believed in those stupidities."

The original is a satirical gem: Syomkina is a suicide because she was expelled from the Party for instability; by committing suicide, Syomkina has proven the Party correct. Syomkina's friend howls as she watches the procession and is praised for her Party discipline—she is a candidate member of the Komsomol—in not participating in the politically anathema rite. But who is it who so admires this Party discipline? It is Mishka-Dobrokhim, just returned from prison. There is no mention of Mishka being an embezzler or having been in prison in the expurgated version.

53   *ached from soccer (bolelo ot futbola)*   In both the collections *Encounters with Lise* (1926) and *The Town of N; Stories* (1989) this is (presumably mistakenly) rendered "gleamed white from soccer" (*belelo ot futbola*).

53   *Comrade Perch*   Many of the names in this story that reverberate with echoes of fruits, animals, and everyday objects, might be perceived as comical. "Mukhin" suggests "fly" (*mukha*), the insect; "Bashmakova" evokes both "shoe" (*bashmak*) and one of Russian literature's best-known characters, Nikolai Gogol's Akakii Akakievich Bashmachkin of "The Overcoat" (1842). "Kapustin" is evocative of "cabbage" (*kapusta*); "Grushkina" hints of "pear" (*grusha*); "Gusev" is both akin to "goose" (*gus'*) and the namesake of a character in Anton Chekhov's eponymous story (1890). Only Comrade Perch's name has been given an English equivalent in

translation, however, as it is the only name that shares identical form with its namesake (*Okun'*).

Mishka-Dobrokhim's moniker is a special case. "Dobrokhim" is not Mishka's surname, but a Soviet acronym identifying Mishka as a member of either the Voluntary Society for Promotion of the Construction of the Chemical Industry (*Dobrovol'noe obshchestvo sodeistviia stroitel'stvu khimicheskoi promyshlennosti*) or the Voluntary Society for the Preparation for Chemical Defense (*Dobrovol'noe obshchestvo po podgotovke k khimicheskoi zashchite*). The irony is that while Mishka is identified in the new Soviet culture by his membership in a "voluntary," or, to be literal, "good-willed" society, the fact is that this "good-willed" character was imprisoned for embezzling from that society.

53   *cultural officer*   In the Russian this is a Soviet acronym, "*kul'trabotnitsa.*"

53   *Volodka Grakov . . . Woldemar*   Katya Bashmakova is in love with Volodka Grakov ("my non-indifference"). Volodka and Woldemar are one and the same person. Both names are variations of Vladimir.

54   *reformatory*   The Russian is another Soviet acronym, "*ispravdom,*" from *ispravitel'no-trudovoi dom* ("corrective labor home").

54   *the obelisk with Comrade Gusev's head on its point*   According to V. S. Bakhtin (*Dobychin-99*, 469), the depiction of the parade and the monument unveiling closely follows an account in a Bryansk newspaper of 1922 of the dedication of a monument to a certain Ignaty Fokin (1889–1919), an organizer of Soviet power in the region.

In "The Nurse," Dobychin interweaves one of the formal ceremonies of the "new" society, with its pompous spectacle and rhetoric, with glimpses of the quotidian world behind official facades. Cinema portraying faraway times and places renders the provincial Soviet reality, despite its parades, dull and bleak by comparison. Grotesqueries of official rhetoric ("The memorial unveiled is a model of monumental art") stand side-by-side with absurdities inflicted on everyday speech ("my non-indifference"). Irreverent humor ("What if that's a skeleton there?") issues from one of the last people who should behave without political correctness. Comrade Perch's comic name mocks the seriousness of her place in society. The funeral procession of a suicide offers real life's answer to the state parade. A perfume display in a shop window evokes unfulfillable dreams. Sunsets, jokes, beer, and sports still adorn the everyday, and the quest for simple human happiness mocks the official world as specious, vicious, and small.

54   *"You fell a victim"*   Words from the *"Funeral March"* (*"Pokhoron-nyi marsh"*), a revolutionaries' song, especially popular after the revolution of 1905 (*Dobychin-99*, 470).

54   *"Tezhe"*   This was the new Soviet name for a store that sells perfume. It is an acronym for the state perfume industry, the State Trust of the Superior Perfumery of the Fats- and Bone-Processing Industry, and an example of the Soviet abandonment of traditional names in favor of no-nonsense, industrial designations. As such, it is a specimen of the *poshlost'*—the self-satisfied vulgarity— Dobychin discerned in the state's treatment of language.

55   *regretted not having brought sunflower seeds*   In *The Town of N; Stories*, "sunflower seeds" (*semechek*) is rendered "little benches" (*skameechek*).

55   *"Mosselprom"*   An acronym for one of the best-known early Soviet industries, the *Moskovskoe ob"edinenie predpriiatii po pererabotke produktov sel'skokhoziaistvennoi promyshlennosti*, or Moscow Association of Enterprises Treating Products of the Agriculture Industry, whose praises famously were sung in couplets by Mayakovsky.

In a letter to an acquaintance Dobychin coquets: "I bought this paper and little envelope in a Mosselprom stall and request that you not judge by their poor quality the qualities of this letter's composer as well" (*Dobychin-99*, 304).

55 *"What do you eat at a desert picnic?"* This punning riddle approximates the one in Dobychin's text, which is based on the phonetic similarity between the phrase *"gde voda dorogá?"* which most listeners will hear as "where is water expensive?" and its tricky twin, *"gde voda da rogá?"* ("where are the water and the horns?"). The answer is: "Horns on the cow, water in the river."

55 *Ukrainian girl* The Russian *"khokhlushka"* is an obsolete colloquial term for Ukrainian (woman), which was originally pejorative, but which had become more jocular at the time in which the story is set. In the variant of "The Nurse" published in *The Town of N; Stories*, *khokhlushka* has been replaced by the intriguing *khokhotushka*, or "titterer."

The Medass

"The Medass" (*"Lekpom"*) was first published, together with the stories "As You Wish" and "Palmistry," in *Leningrad*, no. 3 (1930). The translation is based on the text published in *The Portrait* (1931).

The *Leningrad* publication was prefaced with an editorial caveat, about which Dobychin was to learn only after the fact (*Dobychin-99*, 470): "We are carrying these stories as a typical specimen of the creative work of a petty-bourgeois writer utterly unconnected with our present time. We request readers to speak their minds on the matter of L. Dobychin's stories in the pages of our journal. The editors" (editor's translation).

56 *"Medass"* This is an abbreviation of "medical assistant" and renders the Russian *"lekpom,"* which is an acronym for *lekarskii pomoshchnik* (a medical attendant or physician's assistant, a term coined by the Soviets to replace the traditional term, *"fel'dsher"*). The *fel'dsher* was a common figure in pre-Revolutionary Russian literature.

"Medass" follows the Chekhovian tradition in which "nothing happens," but much is said. If "names" constitute a significant leitmotif in Dobychin's writing, "Medass" occupies a central position, for none of its characters have names, merely social tags, while the two representatives of the world of far away—the Western film stars Mary Pickford and Jenny Jugo—do have names, as if they were somehow more individuated and fully human than these provincials. The "medass" apparently believes that his "interesting life" in town qualifies him to mediate between the village yokels and that distant realm from which movies come. The story incarnates the belief, held by nearly all of Dobychin's characters, that "life is elsewhere."

57   *Mary Pickford*   American film actress (1893–1979), known as "America's Sweetheart," she played spirited heroines in films such as *The Poor Little Rich Girl* (1917).

57   *Jenny Jugo*   Austrian film actress (1905–2001).

The Father

"The Father" ("*Otets*") was first published in the collection *The Portrait* (1931). The translation is based on that text.

The Sailor

"The Sailor" was written in 1926 and first published in *Encounters with Lise* (1927) under the title "Lyoshka." In the collections *The Portrait* (1931) and the unpublished *Material,* Dobychin altered the title to "The Sailor" ("*Matros*"). The translation is based on the text in *The Portrait,* with the exception of a single sentence (see note below), which has been restored from the text in *Encounters with Lise.*

In a letter to M. L. Slonimsky on June 20, 1926, Dobychin writes, regarding "The Sailor" (then titled "Lyoshka"): "There's nothing interesting in it, it resembles a pupil in the higher grades composing according to Classical Models—but to make up for it there aren't any 'politics'" (*Dobychin-99,* 291). In his diary entry of April 29, 1926, Kornei Chukovsky writes: "Received [. . .] a letter from Dobychin. The new story 'Lyoshka' is excellent, but scarcely fit for publication. (He intends it for children)" (*Dobychin-99,* 471).

"The Sailor" anticipates *The Town of N* (1935) in that it is structured around a child's naïve epistemological engagement with his world. As he encounters new phenomena, the child "understands" them by comparing them with phenomena already known to him, which to him they resemble. Thus, the sailor is "brown, like a jug." To wit, this is one of those clay jugs of baked milk he had seen women carrying on yokes that morning. When the sailor's muscles inflate, they resemble the sifted-flour bread the child had seen on Silebina's shelf. So too do the cloudlets, which also appear to be wearing sailors' jackets, such as the one he had seen the sailor wear, as well as resembling heaps of linen, such as those through which he had seen the thieves sorting.

62   *"Transvaal, Transvaal"*   The beginning of a popular song devoted to the Anglo–Boer War of 1899–1902 (*Dobychin-99*, 471). Dobychin evokes the mysterious Transvaal in "The Portrait" as well.

63   *"The poor man's clothes cling to the roots"*   V. S. Bakhtin explains that these are "Lines from the urban (cruel) romance (*gorodskogo [zhestokogo] romansa*) 'The poor girl, killed by grief . . .'" (*Dobychin-99*, 471).

64   *Lyoshka, standing by the water, squished through the mud*   This sentence is missing from the collections *The Portrait* and *Material*.

Palmistry

See note to "The Medass" for publication details of "Palmistry" ("*Khiromantiia*"). The translation is based on the text in *The Portrait* (1931).

65   *"Discharged be the duty that God bequeathed"*   The words of the monk Pimen in Alexander Pushkin's (1799–1837) tragedy *Boris Godunov* (1831).

66   *The Bulgarian woman had died*   A poster advertising a movie that, according to V. S. Bakhtin (*Dobychin-99*, 471), probably concerns the Russian-Turkish War of 1877–78, which resulted in Bulgaria's liberation "from the Turkish yoke."

As You Wish

See note to "The Medass" for publication details of "As You Wish" (*"Pozhaluista"*). The translation is based on the text in *The Portrait* (1931).

68   *"We're already learning May's hymn"*   A song written to the words of "A May Day Song" ("Sing the praises of the Great May Day . . .") by the Proletcult poet Vladimir Kirillov (1890–1943) in 1918 (*Dobychin-99*, 472).

69   *katsaveika*   A short, warm overcoat lined with fur or wadded with cotton.

69   *"I cry and I sob"*   The opening words of a verse from the eighth hymn of the Canon of Saint John of Damascus. They are part of the Eastern Orthodox burial rite (*Dobychin-99*, 472).

The Garden

"The Garden" (*"Sad"*) was first published in the collection *The Portrait* (1931). The translation is based on that text, with corrections following the text in the unpublished *Material*.

70   *Union of Medical Labor Workers*   The Russian is a Soviet acronym, *"medsantrud,"* for *Soiuz rabotnikov mediko-sanitarnogo truda.* Although Dobychin colors many of his stories with examples of the acronyms for institutions and job titles that comprised a major feature of early Soviet culture, he exploits the motif in "The Garden" to farcical effect. The acronyms have not been preserved in the translation, however, since their abundance would render the story incomprehensible. The parade of acronyms would violate the eyes and ears of today's Russian readers nearly as severely as it would their Western counterparts.

70   *Lipetz . . . Lipetzkovaya . . .*   One of Chernyakova's eccentricities is her manner of addressing the poetess and her father by adding

gratuitous suffixes to their family name. Another, which eludes translation, is her reference to the deceased Taisiya not as an *"ubor-shchitsa"* ("cleaning woman"), but as an *"uborshchitsaia"* (a similar looking, but nonexistent word). Dobychin himself enjoyed altering names. In his letters, the writer Elena Mikhailovna Tager is referred to alternately as Tager, Tageriya, and Tagersha. He referred to his own stories by virtually any name other than their actual titles.

71   *office supervisor*   The original is an acronym, *"upravdelami,"* for *upravliaiushchii delami.*

71   *trade union rep*   The original is an acronym, *"profpolnomochennyi,"* for *profsoiuznyi polnomochennyi predstavitel'.*

71   *District Council of Professional Unions*   The original is an acronym, *"okrespeyes,"* for *Okruzhnoi sovet professional'nykh soiuzov (Okr-SPS).*

71   *Union of Education Workers*   The original is an acronym, *"rabot-pros,"* for *Soiuz rabotnikov prosveshcheniia.*

72   *Executive Secretary*   The original is an acronym, *"otsekr,"* for *otvetstvennyi sekretar'.*

72   *District Intersectional Bureau of Engineers and Technicians*   The original is the pronunciation of an acronym, *"okrembeyit,"* for *Okruzhnoe mezhsektsionnoe biuro inzhenerov i tekhnikov.*

72   *key collectionator, a key tillery*   Chernyakova again invents her own language. These are English approximations of her nonsensical improvisations on the words "collector" (*sobiratel'*) and "till" (*kassa*): *soberitel'nitsa* and *kassyia.*

73   *horse artillery division*   The original is an acronym, *"konartdiv,"* for *konno-artilleriiskii divizion.*

73 *sewage disposal men* The original is an acronym, *"assenoboz,"* for *assenizatsionnyi oboz.*

73 *the monument's cloth cap* This is, presumably, a statue of Lenin, the cloth cap being a feature of his official iconography.

73 *"Arise"* The first word of "The International" (see note for "Encounters with Lise").

74 *Department of Culture official* The original is an acronym, *"kul't-otdel'sha,"* for *sotrudnitsa Kul'totdela.*

The Portrait

"The Portrait" (*"Portret"*) was first published in *Stroika*, March 31, 1930. The translation is based on the text in *The Portrait* (1931).

The *Stroika* publication was prefaced with a rather ponderous—and portentous—editorial comment:

> Writer L. Dobychin's unusual method of operation, which has provoked and continues to provoke great controversy, is also of some interest to the general reader who is tracking the paths of development of our contemporary literature and the creative searches of its individual representatives. Proposing to return again to the creative work of L. Dobychin in a special installment, the editorial staff considers it necessary for the time being to make the following proviso: Dobychin's story, very interesting subjectively, objectively—in terms of Soviet literature's current state—signifies much the same thing as the poetry of N. Zabolotsky. The "analytical" perception of the world, breaking down this world into separate "object" details that are as yet unconnected by any organic link, is precisely that characteristic which conceals within itself the danger of a typically bourgeois Weltanschauung of disintegration. This characteristic tendency, typical of an entire group of young writers today, will be subjected in the next issue to a more circumstantial and detailed critique (editor's translation).

According to V. S. Bakhtin (*Dobychin-99*, 473), such a critique apparently never appeared.

75   *"Fyzz-ed"*   This translates the Russian *"fyz'kul'tura,"* which is the landlord's comic mispronunciation of *"fizkul'tura"*—physical education, or phys ed.

75   *earthern mounds (zavalinki)*   These are the earthen mounds that surround Russian peasant huts, serving as protection from the elements and used for sitting out-of-doors.

75   *"Solferino"*   A bright crimson aniline dye, or something colored with or like this dye. The name comes from a northern Italian village where an important battle in the second Italian War of Independence took place on June 24, 1859.

76   *Moscow's Street—formerly Moscow Street*   In a letter of November 17, 1929, to M. L. Slonimsky, Dobychin explains:

> I don't know how to represent this street. Perhaps, to write, *Moscow's (Moskvy)* in full.
>   The idea of this street is that it was simply called Moscow (*Moskovskaia*), but it was renamed on account of the Revolution. No explanations fit into the text, and I've decided to leave it thus (editor's translation).

Dobychin satirizes Soviet officialdom's compulsion to put a revolutionary mark on all aspects of Russian life, no matter how gratuitously. Here a street's name has been altered merely by changing an adjective into a noun (*Moskovskaia ulitsa* to *ulitsa Moskvy*).

76   *church porch*   Apparently the "church" has been deconsecrated and, like so many others, is used as a "Culture Palace" or club.

76   *Richard Tolmedge*   Actually, Talmadge. The American actor (1898–1981) played the romantic lead in some forty feature films in the 1920s and 1930s. Of the twenty-six Talmadge films Dobychin could have seen, none seems to match the scene described in this story. Talmadge films offer, however, the sort of formulaic romance and melodrama that feeds the fantasies of Dobychin's characters. A

caricature of one such melodrama—regarding Miss May and club-man Baybl—appears in "Savkina."

Talmadge's fast-paced films feature the actor's athletic prowess and musculature. They are replete with disguises, coincidences, mistaken identities, and close misses. Their heroes tend to be heirs who must prove they possess character or lower-class boys trying to climb into society. The hero always gets his girl. Titles include *The Wall Street Whiz* (1925), *The Broadway Gallant* (1926), *The Merry Cavalier* (1926), and *The Poor Millionaire* (1930).

Just as Dobychin populates his world with young men ironically tagged "gallants" and "cavaliers," so do those terms recur in Hollywood films of the era. James Joyce's "Two Gallants" (1914), one of the *Dubliners* stories, satirizes the romantic notion of "cavaliers."

77 *the Second International* The International was a federation of working-class political parties whose goal was the transformation of capitalist societies into socialist states, unified in a world federation. Members of the Second International were vilified by Lenin as "opportunists" and "class collaborators" when, at the outbreak of World War I, a majority supported their respective governments' war efforts rather than continuing the class struggle and "transforming the imperialist war into civil war." The Communists organized their own International, the Third International, Comintern, in 1919. The Second International, revived in 1922, became an object of derision in Soviet political culture.

77 *The Poles have taken Polotsk* An episode of the Russo-Polish War of 1919–20.

77 *Anna Chillyag* The creator of a hair growth tonic whose advertisements featured a representation of her standing up, with hair reaching to the ground. These appeared regularly in the newspaper *Dvinsk Listok* for a period of several years (*Dobychin-99*, 473).

77 *Paul Kruger* (Dobychin has *"Kryuger"*) South African statesman (1825–1904). Affectionately known as "Oom (Uncle) Paul," Kruger was president of the Transvaal (South African) Republic

and leader of the Boers from 1883 until the South African (Anglo-Boer) War in 1900. He was popularly regarded as an exotic, romantic figure, largely on the basis of his semiauthentic *Memoirs* (1902), which tell of a youth spent fighting wild beasts, Zulu tribesmen, and rival Boer factions.

77 *"Lunacharsky coshed Rykov"* Anatoly Vasilevich Lunacharsky (1875–1933), revolutionary, writer, and art theoretician, was Education Commissar of the Soviet Union between 1917 and 1929. Aleksei Ivanovich Rykov (1881–1938) was Chairman of the Council of Commissars from 1924 to 1929. Lunacharsky frequently opposed Rykov publicly on matters of policy.

78 *Metropolitan Vvedensky* V. S. Bakhtin (*Dobychin-99*, 473) identifies him as Alexander Vasilevich Vvedensky (1888–1946), a prominent figure in the reform wing of the Russian Orthodox Church, who, in order to save the church, entered into compromise and cooperation with Soviet authorities. He traveled throughout the country, participating in public debates on religious themes with, among others, Lunacharsky.

78 *A sponsored "middle" peasant (podshefnyi serednyak)* This is a "middle" peasant (see definition under "Konopatchikova") who is sponsored by some official Soviet institution in order that, under the guidance of the Communist Party, he become a reliable ally of the proletariat. By the Party's definition, poor peasants were on the side of revolution, while the *kulaks* were enemies. It was over the "middle" peasants that the battle for hearts and minds was waged.

78 *friendship unit (sodruzhestvennaia chast')* A military unit that is under the cultural wardship and tutelage of a Soviet civil institution. This later came to be called a "sponsored unit" (*podshefnaia chast'*), as in the "sponsored 'middle' peasant" above.

79 *"It's quiet all around, and the wind sobs on the knolls"* The opening words of a well-known waltz by I. A. Shatrov (1885–1952), "On the Knolls of Manchuria" (1906), about the 1905 war with Japan.

79   *the Nevsky*   The Nevsky Prospect, the main street in St. Petersburg, then Leningrad.

80   *"In Knopp's store"*   The opening line of an indecent comic verse.

80   *"Christ"*   "Christ has risen!" The Easter procession from church approaches. Aside from its frequent refrain in the Russian Orthodox Eastern Liturgy, "Christ has risen!" is the standard Easter Day greeting.

81   *"Esenin-itis" (eseninshchina)*   Other possible translations include "Eseninistic malady" or "Eseninesque malignity." Sergei Alexandrovich Esenin (1895–1925) was a popular poet, known for his alcoholic debauchery, his raucous marriage to Isadora Duncan, his often sentimental, nationalistic verse, and his suicide at a young age. After his death, Soviet authorities used his name to suggest a certain sort of malaise associated with the poet's tragic vision and celebration of "tavern" life.

      Esenin described himself as "the last poet of wooden Russia." Born into a peasant family, he became disenchanted with the revolution he had welcomed and hanged himself in a Leningrad hotel after writing a last poem in his own blood. Communist critics and Party leaders spoke of the debilitating effect *eseninshchina* exerted on the civic dedication of the young, and Esenin was long out of official favor.

81   *tapping eggs*   In this Easter custom, contestants tap hard-boiled eggs, seeking to break opponents' eggs while maintaining their own intact.

82   *"Damnation to you . . . Mister Trotsky"*   Leon Trotsky's conflicts with Stalin eventually led to his expulsion from the Communist Party. In 1928, the year before "The Portrait" was written, Trotsky was banished from the Soviet Union.

82   *"Violettes de Parme"*   Zhorzhik's hair oil is named after a well-known scent. Oscar Wilde's *The Picture of Dorian Gray* (1891)

instructs that "violets . . . woke the memory of dead romances." Dobychin's "Dorian Gray" portrays a stillborn romance.

82   *"Political slagons?"*   Ivanova misspeaks the Russian word for (political) slogans, saying *"lozguny"* rather than *"lozungi."*

82   *Virineya*   A popular novel (1924) by Lidiya Seifullina (see note to "Lidiya") about a peasant woman ("a mindless rustic") "ripening into a Bolshevik activist, and finally dying a martyr to the cause. One of the earliest 'literary' attempts to show the kind of synthesis that many Marxists at the time believed might result from the conflict of the two great classes [the proletariat and the peasantry]" (Robert A. Maguire, *Red Virgin Soil: Soviet Literature in the 1920s* [Princeton, N.J.: Princeton University Press, 1968], 323–34).

82   *Natalia Tarpova*   A novel (1927–30) by Sergei Semenov (1893–1942).

82   *Poincaré*   Raymond Poincaré (1860–1934), French statesman. Poincaré was Prime Minister and Minister of Foreign Affairs from 1912 to 1913. From 1913 to 1920 he was the ninth President of the third French Republic. *The Great Soviet Encyclopedia* provides the political perspective for Dobychin's story:

> Poincaré represented the interests of the large bourgeoisie. He hindered the passage of social reforms and intensified preparation for war . . . Poincaré was in favor of strengthening the Entente and the alliance with Tsarist Russia, which he visited officially in 1912 and 1914 . . . One of the organizers of intervention in Soviet Russia, he defended the interests of the propertied French in Russia and of the holders of Russian loans . . . From 1922–24, Poincaré was [again] prime minister and minister of foreign affairs . . . In an attempt to increase the power of France in Europe, he sent troops to occupy the Ruhr in 1923."

He was the frequent object of caricatures in the Soviet press. (A different "Monsieur Poincaré" figures in "Kozlova.")

82   *"Proheebited"*   The library attendant places an impossible stress on the third syllable of *"zapreshchena,"* rendering it *"zapreshchyona."*

83   *sovcomworkers*   This renders the early Soviet word, *"sovtorg-sluzhashchie,"* denoting members of the Trade Union of Soviet Government and Trade Employees.

83   *Kabuki*   The Japanese word arose in the late sixteenth century, when Kabuki theater originated. It derived from the verb *"kabuku,"* which applied to anything unusual or curious. The word also carried indecent overtones, probably due to the notorious off-stage conduct of Kabuki performers. It continues to carry this sense of the "unusual" and of the "indecent" in the historical context of "The Portrait." The Japanese "people's theater," Kabuki traditionally offered vivid commentaries on the life of its times, just as "The Portrait" does.

       V. S. Bakhtin, who cites E. Meksh, *"Istoriko-kul'turnyi areal rasskaza L. Dobychina 'Portret'"* (Bakhtin, *Pisatel' Leonid Dobychin,* 273), comments: "In 1928 a tour of a Kabuki theater came through Moscow, and in 1929 there was a trial of a group of leading workers of a construction union who had formed a secret 'Kabuki' society. The goal of the society was to cultivate a 'beautiful life,' 'Athenian nights' with women and wine" (*Dobychin-99,* 474; editor's translation). The trial was well publicized, and "Kabuki" would have carried an aura of lubricious scandal for Soviet citizens of the day. Meksh argues that the scene in "The Portrait" involving Comrade Shatskina and her overburdened cook "is constructed according to the laws of Japanese Kabuki theater, but in a Russian post-Revolutionary-provincial version" (Bakhtin, *Pisatel' Leonid Dobychin,* 274; editor's translation).

84   *jus tollendi*   Latin, "the right to take (away)."

84   *The General*   A classic film comedy (1926) starring Buster Keaton (1895–1966) and set during the American Civil War (1861–65). Keaton portrays a Confederate railroad engineer who pursues Yan-

kee train-nappers. Soviet critics would have preferred Keaton to portray a northerner as the film's hero, since for them the abolitionist Yanks were more correct politically than the slave-owning Confederates.

84   *"Rakhilya"*   V. S. Bakhtin (*Dobychin-99,* 475) suggests that this might be a line from one of the variants of a jocular Odessan song, "Rakhilya, you are beautiful . . ."

84   *"Wishing Citizens to Buy Flowers"*   The original is syntactically and grammatically impossible, likely reflecting its composer's level of literacy.

85   *"begins with a fuh"*   Phosgene (*fosgen*), a most lethal gas.

85   *"Jungsturm" shirt*   An outer shirt of pseudomilitary cut with large pockets, worn with a belt, fashionable in the Communist Youth (*Komsomol*) milieu of the time (*Dobychin-99,* 475).

85   *the Neva and the Fortress*   Pictures of Leningrad, its river, and its Peter and Paul Fortress.

85   *"Our answer to the Chinese generals"*   In 1927–28, Chiang Kai-shek (1887–1975) and his allied warlords of the Kuomintang ("national people's") Party attacked the Communists and the other anti-Chiang factions in the Party, provoking protests and demonstrations in the Soviet Union.

85   *kika*   A traditional Russian headdress worn by married women.

Material

"Material" (*"Mater'ial"*) was written in 1930. Dobychin wanted to include it in *The Portrait* (1931), but it was published only posthumously, in *Leningradskaia pravda,* August 21, 1988. The translation is based on the text published in *Dobychin-99,* 105–6.

In a letter to M. L. Slonimsky on August 31, 1930, Dobychin expressly notes that the "material" referred to in the story's title is not a textile, but "material for purging the organs [of state]" (*Dobychin-99*, 315).

87   *Godulevich received a challenge to a competition*   Dobychin concludes a letter to Slonimsky with words identical to the first two
sentences of this story, except that the librarian to whom he refers
is called Tsukerman (he refers to her as "Tsukermansha"). Tsukerman was the librarian at the Karl Marx Club in Bryansk, where
Dobychin borrowed books. She figures as one of a small group of
acquaintances among Bryansk's citizenry about whom Dobychin,
generally apropos of nothing, relates ironical anecdotes in letters to
fellow writers. Most of these anecdotes implicitly satirize the
absurdities of early Soviet society. In a letter to Kornei Chukovsky
on March 6, 1926, for example, he reports: "I borrowed Fet from
Tsukermansha, in order that afterward I be just like you, only this
Fet is very 'short'—about 45 pages, but, to make up for that, with
pictures (by Konashevich). Tsukermansha resents that she is being
compelled to issue, on deposit of an identity card, eight checkerboards to checkers players, and to watch out that the checkers
aren't stolen." In a letter three days later to Slonimsky and his wife,
Ida Isaakovna, he amplifies Tsukerman's indignation, explaining
that she considers having to concern herself, a librarian, with
checkerboards a "profanation"(*Dobychin-99*, 264). On March 22 of
the same year, Dobychin writes to Chukovsky:

> Dear Kornei Ivanovich. Tsukermansha will be uncommonly
> glad of your greetings. I'll convey them to her as soon as I go to
> return "Arsene Lupen" [Arsène Lupin is the hero of popular
> adventure novels by Maurice Leblanc (1864–1941)—ed.] to her.
> I can just see how she'll blossom and beam.
>
> The roof in her "Karl Marx" leaks and they've put a tub
> under the drips. Several times a minute there resounds a:
> plyukh, plyukh, plyukh—she clutches her head and exclaims,
> "Ugh, how that gets on my nerves!"
>
> Moreover, recently her salary was reduced. I learned of this
> in the following form:
>
> "Tsukermansha swallowed a pill: her salary's been decreased."

She has adorned "Karl Marx's" walls with Slogans: "Read
every day if only for an hour and consider what you've read."
And suchlike.
Of me she asked: "What slogans are there in Leningrad?"—
but I didn't know. (*Dobychin-99*, 265)

In a letter to Slonimsky on March 14, 1927, he notes that he has
already read every book at Tsukerman's "Karl Marx" and that
Tsukerman had asked him, "What's new in the *Spiritual World?*" to
which he replied, "Nothing" (*Dobychin-99*, 284). In a letter to
Slonimsky on March 18, Dobychin returns to Tsukerman's slogans, observing how "to her pique the 'Central Library' is pasting
slogans onto its windows. In the 'Central's' slogans an intoxication
with *conquests* is noticeable: 'The union of the hammer, the sickle,
and the book will conquer the world,' 'Science is the conquest of
religion.' Perhaps this is the success of the work on Militarization
of the Populace" (*Dobychin-99*, 286).

On July 8, 1930, Dobychin reports to Slonimsky that Tsukerman's slogans had landed her in trouble: "Tsukermansha got it hot
for her non-removal of the resolutions of the 16th *partkonferentsiia*
[Communist Party Conference], which are not in fashion now"
(*Dobychin-99*, 311). V. S. Bakhtin (*Dobychin-99*, 525) explains that
at the 16th Party Conference in April 1929 the "optimal variant" of
the First Five Year Plan had been approved and questions concerning agriculture, taxation, and a purging of the Party ranks had been
discussed, but all resolutions had been canceled upon the com-
mencement of Stalin's campaign of forced collectivization of the
peasantry. Tsukerman apparently was too slow in adapting her slogans to match the ill winds of political change.

87   *Closing the library, every evening she would move to the garden . . .*
Compare this with a passage from Dobychin's letter of July 6, 1930,
to Slonimsky:

She In the evening Tsukermansha carries on work outdoors: she
brings to Karl Marx Garden several selected books wrapped in
red cotton textile and, spreading the textile out on a table, lays

out the books on it: those who so desire can read awhile under a lantern, while others watch *Dina Dzadza* [a Soviet film of 1926—ed.] and charm the ladies. A trade union ticket is taken as a deposit. (*Dobychin-99*, 310)

87 *"The Miracles of Shades"* V. S. Bakhtin describes these as "Entertaining little pictures that would change upon examination through varicolored glass; a type of park and home amusement for children in the 1920s and 1930s" (*Dobychin-99*, 475; editor's translation).

87 *venereal hospital* In the Russian this is *"venstatsionar,"* an acronym for *venericheskii statsionar.*

88 *the tsey-eyr-ka* The pronunciation of an acronym that stands for Central Workers' Cooperative (*Tsentral'nyi rabochii kooperativ*).

88 *"Kol Nidrei"* The first two words of the prayer that opens the first evening service of Jewish Yom Kippur. They have come to be taken as the prayer's title. Max Bruch (1838–1920) arranged the traditional Ashkenazi melody for "Kol Nidrei" for cello and orchestra, and it became his most popular work.

89 *an announcement concerning a purge in the communal section* "Purges" were a Soviet phenomenon of the 1920s and 1930s, a form of intimidation and, later, of terror, in which citizens, be they Party officials, trade union members, or the workers of any official institution or enterprise, were subjected to public judgment by their colleagues regarding their political integrity or any relevant character trait, attitude, or performance standard. The consequences of a negative judgment could range from censure to the loss of employment to the loss of civil rights and imprisonment, and helped establish the Stalinist tradition of mass denunciation. Denunciations were motivated by personal enmity, envy, a desire for personal gain (such as being awarded the apartment of the person whom one denounced or a vacation in a government resort), fear of being denounced oneself first, or even by sincerely held ide-

ological beliefs. Denunciations could be based on the mildest of transgressions, such as passing along those humorous couplets about how "Lenin loves kids," which comprise the "material" of Godulevich's intended denunciation. This tradition of "purging" led to the terror of 1936–39, in which millions were condemned to death or incarceration.

90   *live newspaper* A form of amateur show popular in the first decades of the Soviet state in which the members of collectives of all sorts—at factories, resort homes, sports clubs—would perform songs and skits and recite verse concerning social and political issues of the day.

90   *izbas* See note to *izba* under "Yerygin."

Tea

Dobychin first alludes to "Tea" ("*Chai*") in a letter to M. L. Slonimsky dated September 14, 1930, in which he writes: "I've thought up a story about a 'kindergarten.'" It was not published, however, until 1989, in *Zvezda,* no. 9. The translation is based on the text that appears in *Dobychin-99,* 107–8.

91   *friendship unit (sodruzhestvennaia chast')* See note to "The Portrait."

91   *children's playground* The Russian is a Soviet acronym, "*det-ploshchadka.*"

92   *reformatory* See note to "The Nurse."

93   *zhamochki* Round, mint-flavored spice cakes.

93   *tsey-eyr-ka* See note to "Material."

Old Ladies in a Small Town

"Old Ladies in a Small Town" ("*Starukhi v mestechke*") was first published in *Literaturnoe obozrenie*, no. 3 (1988). (The Russian word "*mestechko*" means "small town," but one generally located in Ukraine or Belarus.) It is a variant of an earlier story, "Yevdokiya," which Dobychin also never managed to publish. Dobychin gave the manuscript of "Old Ladies in a Small Town" to Veniamin Kaverin, who preserved it until it could be published, more than half a century later. The translation is based on the text in *Dobychin-99*, 423–30.

95   *art. Tsyperovich (khud. Tsyperovich)*   Readers of *The Town of N* (1935) will recognize this "small town" as that to which Alexandra Lvovna Lei moves after winning two hundred thousand in the lottery. All the town's shop signs have been painted and signed by the artist Tsyperovich. "Old Ladies in a Small Town" shares numerous characters and details with *The Town of N*. Katerina Alexandrovna, who is snubbed by the Countess and seeks revenge through an anti-Polish campaign, and who goes each day to the top of a hill to contemplate her will, is in some ways a prototype for Alexandra Lvovna Lei.

95   *"Bridge Dangerous"*   The same sign appears near the end of "The Portrait."

95   *a girl . . . holding a pillowslip stretched on a frame over her head*   The same child appears in "Lidiya."

95   *cobblestone fence*   This fence (*zabor*) becomes a wall (*stena*) six paragraphs later.

97   *"When my Karlchen was alive, he was treating them at the palazzo, then I also with them was acquainted. But when they showed me their fanatismus, then I no more with them am acquainted"*   Frau Anna makes numerous mistakes in Russian, which is not her native tongue. Not all of her poor Russian is preserved in the 1989 collection.

97   *"A tempestuous wind, called Euroclydon"*   See Acts 27:14.

98   *Roman Catholic church*   Katerina Alexandrovna, like most Russians of the time, belongs to the Eastern (Russian) Orthodox faith, and it is from a Russian Orthodox Mass in a Russian Orthodox church (*tserkov'*) that she is returning with Dashenka and Hieretiida. The church in front of which the sleigh from the palazzo stands is a Roman Catholic church—a *kostyol*—and the Countess Anna, like most Poles, belongs to the Roman Catholic faith. Snubbed by the Countess in this scene, Katerina Alexandrovna will use this difference in nationality and religion in her efforts to excite antagonism toward her.

101   *The Reading Circle (Krug chteniia)*   A compendium of edifying readings (1904–8) for each day of the year, culled by Lev Tolstoy (1828–1910) from the writings of various cultures.

101   *Herod was having a bite to eat with guests . . . The sliced-through neck of Saint John was red on the inside with little white circles, like the sausage on a Tsyperovich sign*   Dobychin rehearses this biblical scene with even more blood and gusto in *The Town of N:*

> We saw Herod, before whom danced his fat-cheeked stepdaughter, hands propped against her sides. I thought that thus, perhaps, had Sophie once danced before her stepfather. John the Baptist's head lay on a tablecloth amid loaves and cups, while his body lolled in the corner. His neck, seen in section, was dark red with a whitish dot in the middle. Blood spurted in an arc (editor's translation).

101   *Katerina Alexandrovna, waiting for them by the entrance, was eating the host*   The Russian word *"pritvor,"* translated here as "by the entrance," is the space inside a Russian church nearest the entrance. The narthex of Western church architecture might be a suitable approximation.

101   *a greenish little old man . . . Gorokhov*   Gorokhov, whose name
derives from the Russian word for pea (*gorokh*), is either appropriately named or appropriately tinted.

101   *Saint Alexander Nevsky*   Perhaps Russia's greatest hero (1220–
63), Alexander was a warrior-monk whose legend has been ideal-
ized by chroniclers over the centuries, often by conflation with the
life of Alexander the Great. As Prince of Novgorod, he earned his
surname by defeating the Swedes on the Neva River in 1240. He
subsequently defeated the Livonian (Teutonic) Knights (1242) and
the Lithuanians (1245), and later reigned as Grand Duke of
Vladimir-Suzdal. He is the patron saint of St. Petersburg.

101   *Tsarskoe Selo*   Situated fifteen miles south of St. Petersburg, the
"Tsars' Village" is the location of the imperial palaces and parks of
empresses Elizabeth Petrovna (1709–61) and Catherine II
(1729–96). It became known as a summer resort for aristocratic and
wealthy families in the nineteenth century and was renamed "Det-
skoe selo" ("Children's Village") and, later, "Pushkin" during
Soviet times.

102   *"what if that's a skeleton there?"*   Compare with "The Nurse,"
where Comrade Perch makes the same coquettish joke.

103   *"You're ambling along the companies and see the blue cupola with
stars"*   See the note for "In the companies" for "Encounters with
Lise." The blue cupola belongs to the enormous Trinity Cathedral
on Izmailovsky (later, Krasnoarmeisky) Prospect in St. Petersburg.

103   *"Dragging themselves along toward the Warsaw Station are hay carters
with baskets at their feet"*   The 1989 Dobychin collection has
"sleepy carters" (*sonnye izvozchiki*).

103   *"Anna, Anna, you didn't want me to draw back the curtain"*   Katerina Alexandrovna silently appeals to Countess Anna here, not to
her neighbor, Frau Anna Frantsevna Rabe, or her acquaintance,

Anna Ivanovna. The plethora of characters named "Anna" in this story is intriguing.

103   *Saint John's Day*   St. John the Baptist's Day or Midsummer Day (*Ivanov den'* or *Ivan-Kupala*) is observed on June 24, Old Style.

104   *physharmonium (fisgarmonium)*   In "Yevdokiya" this musical instrument is called a "physharmonica" (*fisgarmoniia*). The physharmonica is a free-reed, keyboard instrument with compression bellows and a span of four octaves. Shaped like a small, low table, it is akin to the harmonium.

105   *"War's been declared"*   Germany declared war on Russia on August 1, 1914.

105   *"Over there, some beefy guys are bathing without hollering"*   A close variant of this line appears in "Savkina," part 3: "Two beefy guys [*verzili*] were bathing—and without hollering [—*i ne gorlanili*]." One is tempted to see them as the same two beefy guys, still quietly bathing in the same river ten years later.

105   *"God keep the tsar"*   See note to "God, Tsar" for "Encounters with Lise."

Ninon

"Ninon" was written in either 1923 or early 1924, but not published until 1989 (*Zvezda*, no. 9). The translation is based on the text that appears in *Dobychin-99*, 335–37.

Dobychin apparently lost faith in "Ninon." In a letter of December 27, 1924, he reacts to criticism Kornei Chukovsky directed at several of his stories: "I won't stand up for 'Ninon,' but do You find all the rest to be over-dried as well?" In a letter to M. L. Slonimsky (February 10, 1925), he writes: "I don't like 'Ninon' either. Please, don't print it." The story is nevertheless a favorite of readers today (*Dobychin-99*, 252 and 270).

A light homosexual motif runs through Dobychin's writing, most notably in *The Town of N* (1935). The stories contain, at the least, signs of

sexual ambiguity, ranging from the cavaliers dancing with cavaliers and ignoring the maidens in "Dorian Gray"—the name of a novel by one of history's most famous homosexuals—to firemen dancing with firemen in "The Father" and "aunts" dancing with "aunts" in "Tea." Barb's mustache and beard recall Zaitseva's mustaches in "Lidiya." The eponymous "Lidiya" is the name of a nanny goat that formerly had been called "Georgie." In "Farewell," Kunst recoils at the slightest display of female sexuality. In "Tea," Kolya falls in love with Misha and is jealous when Misha chooses to dance with a female partner, while Shaikina and Porokhonnikova apparently wish to steal away to be alone in the dark.

107   *Marie (Mari)*   Marie is Marya Petrovna's nickname.

110   *Varenka (Varen'ka)*   Both Barb and Varenka are diminutives of the name Varvara; they are one and the same person.